"Take some time to weigh the pros and cons."

Royce stood casually, at his back the sunlit skyline of Toronto, on his lips a slight coaxing smile.

"Think about it, Jenna. I need a wife. We won't pretend there's any love between us, but I know we could get on together. I'll provide for you and your child. You'll be paid well. And in return you'll care for my family and home as efficiently as you do the office."

It was the most cold-blooded proposition Jenna had ever heard.

"There's nothing to think about," she said abruptly. "The answer is no."

His expression darkened.

"Don't be so quick to refuse. You'll have to look long and hard before you find another man who'll accept your illegitimate son with no questions asked."

Books by Maura McGiveny

HARLEQUIN PRESENTS
674—A GRAND ILLUSION

HARLEQUIN ROMANCES
2511—DUQUESA BY DEFAULT

These books may be available at your local bookseller.

For a free catalog listing all titles currently available,
send your name and address to:

Harlequin Reader Service
P.O. Box 52040, Phoenix, AZ 85072-2040
Canadian address: Stratford, Ontario N5A 6W2

MAURA MCGIVENY

a grand illusion

Harlequin Books

TORONTO • NEW YORK • LONDON
AMSTERDAM • PARIS • SYDNEY • HAMBURG
STOCKHOLM • ATHENS • TOKYO • MILAN

Harlequin Presents first edition March 1984
ISBN 0-373-10674-2

Original hardcover edition published in 1983
by Mills & Boon Limited

CHAPTER ONE

JENNA finished the last line of the page she was typing and pulled the paper from her typewriter before glancing at the clock. In five more minutes another working day would be done. She rubbed the back of her neck and let a small tired sigh escape her.

The other girls in the typing pool had finished at least fifteen minutes earlier and sat at their desks with their coats on, their faces freshly made up, their eyes on the clock. Talking back and forth, they were full of the latest gossip about the recently hired illustrator, but Jenna felt set apart from them somehow. Not that she wanted to be, it just always happened that way. Turning a deaf ear, she let the conversation wash over her as she began to straighten the pile of papers on her desk.

'He's so gorgeous!' one of the girls gushed.

'I hear he's a very eligible bachelor. Imagine, handsome and kind too,' someone else chimed in.

Elaine, the girl whose desk was nearest Jenna's, smiled dreamily, her plump face glowing. 'I can't imagine going out with him. I'd probably be so tongue-tied, I'd just sit and look into his beautiful eyes all evening.' She laughed lightly. 'What would you do, Jenna?'

She looked up at the mention of her name. 'Were you talking to me?'

Elaine grimaced and then all the others started to laugh as they filed out of the room.

'Isn't that just like her?'

'I don't think she knows what's going on half the time.'

'Chad Redwicke's been here a week already and she's the only one in the whole building who hasn't made a play for him . . .'

Their voices drifted away, then there was only silence.

Jenna straightened the cover on her typewriter with a sigh and reached in the bottom drawer for her handbag. She was buttoning her coat before she noticed the man standing in the doorway watching her.

The girls were right. He was handsome. His hair was blond and slightly waving, his face tanned, his eyes a dark velvety brown as they roamed over her.

'Did you want something, Mr Redwicke?' she asked quietly.

'Yes, Jenna.' He smiled, coming closer. 'I want you . . .' Letting his words hang expectantly in the air, waiting for her reaction, he was disappointed when nothing was forthcoming. 'May I drive you home?' he asked with a touch of dented ego.

The faintest tinge of red crept into her face. 'Thank you, but no, I'd really rather walk.'

'All I'm asking for is the pleasure of your company for an hour or so. I'll take you home and if you like, you can change and then we'll go somewhere for a drink, have a nice quiet little dinner.' He turned on his most charming smile showing his perfect white teeth.

She spoke softly, with a shy smile, but remained firm in her refusal. Her step was light when she turned away from him and started towards the door. 'Thanks anyway, Mr Redwicke. Maybe some other time.'

'There won't be any other time and you know it.' His face changed, all pretence of charm vanishing. 'Does it give you some kind of thrill to have refused every man in this building?'

Jenna stiffened, turning back to him, struggling to keep her voice calm. 'I'm sure I don't know what you mean.'

'Oh yes, you do. You've heard the office gossip. "Iceberg", they call you. Every one of the men have tried, but they can't get you to accept even the most innocent offer of a lift home. I'm new here, but I haven't got leprosy. Why won't you let me take you home?'

'Please don't take it personally,' she said quietly. 'I appreciate your offer, but I enjoy the walk. Now that spring's almost here, I'd like to take advantage of the nice weather.' She looked at him leaning negligently against the filing cabinet and sighed, knowing he wasn't the type who took no for an answer.

'That's not it, Iceberg,' he jeered. 'There's something you're trying to hide, and we all wonder what it is. What's at home you don't want anybody to know about? I've got an open mind. You can tell me.'

Jenna's chin shot up. She wasn't exactly ashamed of her home life, but she didn't go around flaunting it either. Her eyes flashed a bitter blue, but she managed to keep her voice steady. 'I don't have to explain myself to you. I've refused your offer in the most gracious way I know. The least you could do is accept it without indulging in idle speculation and repeating distorted gossip.'

His lip curled as he straightened and held the door for her. 'You're scaring men away, Jenna, and a plain girl your age can't afford to do that. What's the deep dark secret hiding under all that ice?'

His remarks were meant to sting, but Jenna, more than anybody else, knew she was plain, and her manner did scare men away, so he didn't hurt as much as he might have done. She was short and slender, with plain mouse brown hair and unremarkable blue eyes. Always neat and clean, she didn't wear make-up or the latest fashions, and as a result, she tended to blend into the woodwork. People always thought she was older than her twenty-three years and she never corrected them. Extremely shy, she gave the impression of being standoffish, but she didn't know how to overcome it.

Without answering him, she lifted her chin and walked swiftly towards the time clock, but before she was out of earshot she heard one of the other men from the graphic department chortle: 'You lose the bet, old boy. I told you she wouldn't go with you!'

The watery rays of the April sun filtered across the Toronto skyline, and Jenna shivered as she made her way down Yonge Street. The cold didn't bother her, but her thoughts did. She shook them off with an effort. This was her time of day and nothing would spoil it. Walking home like this, the only thing she allowed to make demands on her was the traffic signals. For three-quarters of an hour she could let her mind wander, forgetting all her obligations. The wind tugged at her topknot and her hair loosened, whipping across her face. She smiled widely, the first time that day, a light airy smile of relief.

Almost spring, she kept telling herself. Soon the wind would be warm and gentle. Flowers would be everywhere. And sunshine—oh yes, hot, healing sunshine. She almost floated down the last two blocks to her home, but long before she reached the snug, comfortable, run-down house that had been converted into a two-family flat, she heard the strident cries.

Stumbling up the sidewalk, she found her key and let herself in. 'Meg? I'm home!' She dropped her coat on a chair just inside the door and quickly walked to the bedroom where a tall blonde girl was bent over a cot. 'What on earth——?'

'Thank God you're home!' The girl straightened and ran a distracted hand through her tousled hair. 'He's been crying like this ever since you left this morning. For two cents I'd strangle him!'

Jenna looked at the tiny baby. His face was flushed and his nose was running and his eyes were red and puffy. 'Does he have a fever?' she asked.

'I don't know.'

'What do you mean, you don't know? Didn't you take his temperature?'

'Don't make it sound like such a crime! I don't even know how.'

Jenna pressed her lips together and walked to the bathroom. When she came back she was shaking down a thermometer. 'I'll show you. In case this happens again.'

'I don't want to know.'

'Meg! Don't you have any feeling for him? He's sick.'

'Listen, sister dear, he's your responsibility. You wanted him, not me. I only wanted to be free, to do what I like, live my own life, be able to go places without being stuck with a crying brat. Think back to the way things were before he came. They could be that way again if only you'd get rid of him. Put him up for adoption, that's the easiest thing to do.'

Jenna closed her eyes and counted to ten, then pushed Meg out of the bedroom. 'Go and put the kettle on for me, will you? I'll take care of Robbie.'

With ill grace, Meg flounced out. 'Don't be long. I have a very important date tonight.'

Jenna bit back a ready retort and gathered Robbie into her arms. 'Okay, little boy,' she murmured soothingly, 'Auntie's here. What seems to be the trouble?'

He rubbed his eyes with his tiny fists and clung to her, whimpering softly.

Nearly half an hour later Jenna found her sister in the bathroom putting the finishing touches to her make-up. 'He's asleep,' she said quietly. 'His temperature's up, but he's not wheezing much. I think it might be his teeth and not the bronchitis this time.'

'Spare me the gory details,' Meg said callously.

'How can you be this way?' sighed Jenna hopelessly.

'I told you before, I wasn't the motherly type. All that rot about instinct——' Meg tossed her head in exasperation. 'We've been all through this before. When are you going to accept it? I'll never be a mother to that boy. It's bad enough having to babysit all day until I can find work. I knew I never should have had him. I didn't want him before, and I don't want him now. All he's done for the last six months is cause problems.'

'And Peter?' Jenna's voice was hard and inflexible.

'You leave Peter out of this!' Meg rounded on her. 'He doesn't know anything about him, and that's the way I want it. The only thing that interests him is ancient cities buried under tons of earth. Nothing else matters to him.'

'But don't you think he has a right to know after all this time? Robbie's his son too.'

Meg splashed on some expensive cologne and fluffed the ends of her carefully dyed blonde hair. 'I couldn't drop a bombshell like that on him. He's married, remember? If you knew him, you'd know it would only cause complications. His wife would never let him live it down. Besides, his brother wouldn't tolerate any kind of scandal connected with the almighty Drummond name. He'd probably cut off Peter's allowance, and since he can't abide children either, he'd insist on blackballing me from every modelling agency in town and taking the kid away from you. Is that what you want? I thought you promised Mom you'd always take care of me?'

Jenna looked at her for a long distraught moment, wondering for the umpteenth time how such a beautiful girl could be so callous, then shook her head, knowing it was useless. It shouldn't have surprised her that Meg wouldn't grow up and start being responsible for herself, but it always did.

Running her fingers over her skin-tight skirt and smoothing the two wisps of deep blue chiffon that made up the top of her evening dress, Meg smiled into the mirror. 'How do I look?'

Jenna bit her lip hard to prevent a rebuke from rushing out. 'It's a bit daring, isn't it?' she managed.

'Only you would say that! I'm a model, not a nun. I've got to prove I've got the qualifications, and telling them isn't enough. They've got to see for themselves. Nobody knows I was pregnant and they won't be able to tell by looking at me. I'm going to the top of my profession!'

'Oh, Meg, why don't you give it up?' Exasperation made Jenna's voice husky. 'I make enough money to keep us comfortable. If we're careful——'

'You don't really believe that?' Meg sneered sarcastically. 'It's all right for you to keep wearing the same clothes year after year, but I need new ones—lots of new ones. There's never enough money for the things I have to have. You're only thinking of yourself, making us live like this. There's nothing for me here, no glamour, no action, no excitement. Nothing to do.'

Jenna's eyes swept around the cluttered flat and then stopped accusingly on Meg. 'You could at least pick up after yourself. That would give you something to fill your time.'

'I'm off, little mother,' Meg said quickly, ignoring the grim line of her sister's mouth. 'Don't wait up for me. I'm hoping I'll be late!'

The expensive scent Meg used lingered long after she had gone, and Jenna sighed, feeling drained now that she was alone. Meg was so vibrant and alive and glowing. When she left she seemed to take everything exciting with her. Meg was right, there was no glamour or action here. Just the same old dull routine.

She ate a small inelegant meal of tinned soup and managed to restore the flat to order and cleanliness before she checked again on the baby and retired for the night. But just after she had dozed off, Robbie started to cry, and she hurried in to him.

'There, there,' she murmured, picking him up and rocking him gently, trying to soothe him, 'your other mother's here and everything's going to be all right.'

It took more than two hours to settle him and then she heard a key in the door and Meg's light tinkling laugh. Yawning tiredly, Jenna waited a few minutes to allow her some privacy and give her enough time to say goodnight to whoever brought her home.

But when she started back to her own room, she heard Meg's slightly slurred voice and the coaxing deeper masculine tones trying to wear down her resistance.

'No, I can't ask you in for coffee. My sister's probably asleep.'

'I wouldn't wake her. I've heard she needs all the beauty sleep she can get. Just five minutes, Meg. For old times' sake?'

'I really shouldn't, Royce, but—all right. Five minutes.'

'No, Meg,' said Jenna in a low quiet voice,

standing in the shadows of the small living room. 'Not five minutes—not even five seconds.'

'Jenna! What are you doing up?' Meg flicked on a lamp and pinned her with an angry glare. 'Spying on me?'

She glanced at the tall man standing behind Meg and her face hardened. Arrogance was blatant in every line of his erect posture as he stood looking at her. He was striking, with thick black hair and finely chiselled features. Two deep grooves dented the sides of his handsome face and there was a deep dimple in his chin. With a sudden curling in the pit of her stomach, she wondered again where Meg always managed to find such gorgeous creatures. She'd never find one like him in a million years. 'You should know better,' she said quietly, forcing her to remember past indiscretions.

Meg's sudden whitening at the reminder made Jenna sigh in apology.

'I wasn't spying. I was up because Robbie was awake.'

'Oh.' Meg dismissed that information as inconsequential and turned to the man. 'Sorry, Royce, I'll have to say goodnight now.'

'Not yet.' He took several long strides into the room and flicked a contemptuous look at Jenna standing in her bare feet and faded blue bathrobe, her brown hair hanging in sleep-tangled disorder far down her back. 'I'm sure your sister realises you're old enough to invite a man in for a nightcap if you want to. Won't you introduce me? And who's Robbie?'

Meg suddenly seemed to dwindle right before Jenna's eyes. 'My sister, Jennifer,' she whispered chokingly. 'This is Royce Drummond.'

Jenna's eyes widened and she gripped the folds of her robe in front of her in an unconsciously protective gesture. *'Peter's brother?'* It was out before she could stop the words from forming.

'You know him?' His slashing grey gaze swept over her, and she felt a shock of fear race down her spine.

'Of course she knows him,' Meg interrupted, her voice breathless. 'And now you'd better go— Jenna has to get up early for work tomorrow.'

At first Jenna thought he was going to leave, but he merely turned back to the door and closed it quietly.

'Who's Robbie?' he asked.

Meg swallowed. 'Nobody——'

'—Nobody you need be concerned about,' Jenna said smoothly, somehow finding her voice and successfully drawing his attention away from Meg. 'Robbie's my little boy.'

'You have a son!'

A certain grimness stole over her face and her mouth hardened. 'Yes, Mr Drummond. Even plain girls—who need all the beauty sleep they can get—have sons.'

The grey sheen of his eyes slid over her thoughtfully, taking in her tumbled hair and the slim rigid length of her body in the faded bathrobe. She had a dignity in her anger that astounded him. He inclined his head and smiled an apology with effortless charm. 'I'm sorry you heard me say that. I had no idea you were married or that you had a son. My brother spoke of Meg's sister in a very different light.'

'I'm sure he must have,' she said with clipped

finality, brushing past him to open the door. 'Goodnight, Mr Drummond.'

He had no choice but to leave, and after a slight hesitation, he nodded regretfully to Meg and left them.

After he had gone, Jenna turned to her sister and couldn't contain her anger. 'How dare you!'

'Please, Jenna!' begged Meg.

'Don't you "please, Jenna" me! That was Peter's brother! How could you? Don't you realise what could have happened? We were just talking about it before you left.'

'I couldn't help it.'

Jenna swallowed convulsively. 'But you invited him in! Don't you have any sense at all? What if he'd seen Robbie? You told me he knew how thick you and Peter were. What if he'd recognised him?'

'But he didn't. Lots of babies have black hair and cleft chins, not just the Drummond family. Besides, it wasn't my fault he brought me home. Andrew Lawford couldn't make it. He asked Royce to meet me instead. I was just as surprised as you.' Meg pouted prettily. 'We had dinner and talked over old times. Royce is really handsome, isn't he? I never realised it before. I always thought he was so much older than Peter, but thirty-three isn't all that old, is it? Pretty soon I'll be twenty. And did you know Peter's getting a divorce?'

Jenna threw up her hands in exasperation. 'Meg, don't you have any sense? Can't you understand how serious this is? If you start entertaining thoughts of Peter Drummond again or his brother, what's it going to mean to your son?'

'I knew I never should have had that baby,' Meg wailed. 'There's been nothing but trouble ever since he was born. I never should have let you talk me into keeping him. He's not my son! He's yours. You even said so. You wanted him, not me. As soon as I can, I'm geting away from here. I'm going to be a famous model and be rich and have a string of wealthy husbands——'

'Oh, go to bed!' Jenna shouted. 'You make me sick!'

She was late for work the next day. Chad Redwicke was standing by the time clock in the hallway outside the typing pool and got the full blast of her icy stare.

'Mr Farnsworth's been looking for you, Iceberg,' he said with a sneer. 'You've kept him waiting nearly half an hour now. Don't be surprised if he gives you the sack. He's been asking some pretty personal questions about you lately.'

Jenna didn't stop to worry about his spiteful speculations but quickly ran the length of the corridor to the executive offices and knocked softly on the door before going in.

'Mr Farnsworth was wondering why you were keeping him waiting, Jenna,' his pretty young secretary said with a slight frown. 'It's not at all like you to be so late for work. Go right in.'

Without giving herself a chance to be frightened of this summons, she pushed open the door and noiselessly walked toward the massive leather-topped desk. 'Mr Farnsworth?'

'Ah, Miss Caldwell. Come in, come in, my dear. Take off your coat and sit down.'

He was a tall thickset man with pure white hair and a beaming smile. It was the first time Jenna had ever seen him, although she had heard about him often enough and his signature was on all her pay-cheques.

He waved to a brown leather chair in front of his desk. 'I've heard some very good things about you. Thank you for coming.'

She hated the betraying colour that rose to her face, but she didn't say anything. Her hands began to twist nervously in her lap as Mr Farnsworth continued to look at her. Forcing herself to at least look relaxed, Jenna leaned back in her seat and looked straight into his assessing eyes. If he was waiting for an explanation for her tardiness, he was going to be disappointed. How could she tell him she had been up the entire night with a sick baby? There was nothing she could say to him that wouldn't involve long explanations of her complicated home life, and so far she had kept home and work separated. It was going to stay that way.

'A very unusual girl,' he murmured. 'And I've heard you can keep a secret. Can you, Miss Caldwell?'

She blinked, frowning. 'I've never really thought much about it.'

'Ah.' He smiled with evident satisfaction and leaned forward in his chair. 'I have a secret for you. I'm retiring—and so is my secretary.'

Jenna forced a small smile to her bewildered face, wondering why he was telling her.

'We're getting married.'

'Oh!' Her face fell, but she recovered herself instantly. It was none of her business if he was going to marry a woman thirty years his junior. 'Why, congratulations—to both of you. I wish you every happiness.'

'Thank you, my dear.' He rubbed his hands together and nodded. 'You'll do very nicely, very nicely indeed!'

Jenna sat helplessly, looking at him in silence, wondering where all this was leading.

'You might have heard the rumours, that this company is being absorbed by another advertising agency?'

She nodded.

'Within a week you'll have a new boss—and I've chosen you to be his executive secretary. With a very substantial raise in pay, of course.'

'Me? But why?' She was shocked and her mouth started to fall open, but she caught it just in time and snapped it shut.

Mr Farnsworth smiled complacently. 'You just passed the test"

Her eyebrows rose.

'Yes, my dear. You kept me waiting, but the minute you came in here you didn't start explaining and apologising all over the place. And you don't have to think about keeping a secret—it comes naturally. And even though I shocked you with my announcement, you had the presence of mind to congratulate me and wish me happiness. You're a woman of few words. I like that—very much. And so will your new boss. I've heard he can't abide frivolous women. That's why I had to be very careful in my selection of a secretary for him. I was told to find a paragon.'

Jenna let out her breath slowly, not realising she had been holding it. 'Then you've chosen the wrong person, Mr Farnsworth. I don't consider myself able to meet such a standard of excellence.'

'You're merely expected to do your job to the best of your very considerable ability, my dear. I've seen your work and I've watched you when you weren't aware of it. I've talked to your co-workers, and nobody seems to know anything about you. You're very wise, keeping your own counsel. Not many young women these days can do that. Let's see, this is Friday. On Monday morning you're to report to my secretary. She'll show you the ropes, so to speak.' He chuckled to himself. 'She used those ropes to tie me to her side very neatly!'

A reluctant smile crossed her face and he beamed at her. 'You have a sense of humour too, I see. A pity you don't use it more. I'm afraid you'll be called on to use it often after next Friday.'

'Is the job that difficult?'

'The job, no. The boss, yes. Royce Drummond runs a tight ship.'

'Royce Drummond!' gasped Jenna.

'Do you know him?'

It was a good thing Jenna was sitting down, because she might have fallen over in shock. 'I've met him,' she said in a choking whisper.

'Wonderful. Then I don't have to feel quite so guilty feeding you to the lions.'

And that was just what he'd be doing, she realised. 'Mr Farnsworth, I'm sorry, but I can't possibly take this job,' she told him.

'Of course you can.' He waved away her objections with a wide smile. 'You're extremely well qualified.'

Her teeth mangled her bottom lip as she sat looking at him. All kinds of conflicting thoughts chased through her mind, throwing her into confusion, but one thought became uppermost, and that was the realisation that she'd have to find a new job within a week. There was no way she could continue working in the same building as Royce Drummond, let alone become his secretary and work in the same office!

'Before you tell me no again,' he beamed, 'let me point out to you that you were hand-picked from a field of five prospective employees. Your typing and short hand are top-notch, as theirs is. You're clean and neat and punctual, as they are. But the thing that tipped the scales so heavily in your favour is the fact that you don't rush to leave the building at quitting time. That's very rare. You have every qualification I was told to find.'

'You're very flattering, sir, and I do thank you, but I really can't——'

He held up his hands to stop her. 'I've probably caught you off guard. Please, take this weekend to think about it. Think very carefully what this promotion will mean in terms of advancement as well as money. And remember, an opportunity like this may never again come your way. We'll talk again on Monday morning.' His smile was wide and complacent as he walked her to the door, patting her shoulder gently.

When she returned to the typing pool all the other girls were agog with curiosity, but Jenna didn't satisfy it. She quickly buried herself in her work and tried to push the whole conversation out of her mind until she could find the time to devise a plan. The only thing certain was that she couldn't work here any longer. It was too dangerous. If he ever saw Robbie . . .

The afternoon flew and when she got home that night she didn't have to look for something to take her mind off Mr Farnsworth's impossible offer. Robbie was definitely ill and she had no time to think of anything else.

'Meg, why didn't you ring me this afternoon?' she said accusingly, sponging Robbie's hot, flushed body and trying to calm his sobs. 'If you didn't want to take him to a doctor yourself, I'd have come home and done it.'

'You don't get paid for the time you take off,' she shrugged. 'You had to spend a lot of money on all that special formula for him last week, and I wasn't about to have you take time off and then say we couldn't afford that skirt and sweater you promised me this week.'

Jenna gritted her teeth and eyed the pink cashmere dress draping Meg's supple figure. It was relatively new, having been bought three months ago when she had regained her pre-natal measurements. Jenna hadn't had anything new for the last year and a half, but she swallowed back the tightness in her throat and put Robbie back in his cot. 'You'll have the money for the clothes, Meg,' she said quietly. 'I'll see if I can get a doctor to come out to the house, or I may have to take him to the Emergency Room at the hospital.'

'It's probably not that bad.' Meg peered into the mirror and blotted her lipstick. 'You told me yourself it's probably just teething pains.'

'It's got to be more than that. I just know it.

He's wheezing and his fever's so high he's starting to dehydrate.'

'He had some water this afternoon, but he didn't want any of the formula, so I thought you'd give it to him when you came home.'

Jenna nodded and phoned the doctor. By the time she had finished her call, Meg was standing by the door with her coat on.

Before she could say anything, Meg rushed into an explanation. 'I'm going out with Royce tonight—and don't tell me I can't! You don't have to worry about him coming in, though. You were successful in freezing him out last night, and he doesn't want to risk running into you again.' And then she was gone, as a car horn sounded in the street.

Grimacing to herself, Jenna walked back to Robbie's room and didn't waste her energy wishing Meg could be different. Meg was Meg. She had always been self-centred. It shouldn't make her heart twist so painfully each time she realised this baby meant absolutely nothing to her. She had gambled on motherly instinct and lost. It was just something she'd have to accept.

Within the hour a doctor came. He was middle-aged and plump with keen dark eyes and a crisp comforting manner. His examination was thorough, and when he snapped his black bag shut, his expression was serious.

'Is there a history of asthma in your family?'

Jenna shook her head, frowning. 'Not that I can recall. My parents both died in a boating accident last year, but before that they were always in good health.'

'What about the baby's father?'

She looked at him blankly. She had never met Peter, and Meg had never really told her anything about him except that he was married and that he was interested in archaeology.

'You do know who the father is?' he prodded.

Brilliant colour ran into her face as she bit back the explanation that she wasn't Robbie's mother. 'Yes, I do. But I don't know if there's any asthma in his family and there's no way I can contact him to find out.'

He sighed. 'Then for now I'll diagnose it as a severe case of bronchitis. I'll give you some antibiotics and check him again tomorrow.'

'Do you think he should go to hospital?' she asked.

'Not yet. Let's see how he responds to a change of formula as well as this medication, hm?'

Several hours later, when Robbie had finally drifted off to sleep, Jenna sat at the kitchen table with a pencil and paper, dividing her pay-cheque into small amounts, trying to make it stretch far enough to cover the new soybean milk formula for Robbie and the cost of a new skirt and sweater for Meg.

If she got up earlier and walked to work as well as home again instead of taking the bus, it would save a little. She crossed that off her list. If the electricity company was at all understanding, they might let her take an extra week to pay this month's bill without a penalty. The rent was already a month overdue and the landlady was beginning to make grumbling noises every time she saw her in the hallway so she couldn't put that off any longer. Try as she might, there was no way to make ends meet.

There is a way, a small insistent voice nagged at her.

No, she argued with herself. The risk is too great. I can't take a chance on losing Robbie.

But you've been able to keep home and work separate so far, the more daring part of her mind persisted. And it's obvious you're not Royce Drummond's type, so you don't have to worry about him getting personal. Why not try it? You can always quit if you see it isn't going to work out. You won't know if you don't try.

We do need the money, her practical side conceded. And Robbie could have all those extra little things I haven't been able to get for him.

A troubled smile crossed her strained white face. Royce Drummond asked for a paragon, did he? Wait till he sees who it is!

She pushed the small pile of money aside, clearing a space, and dropped her head on her arms, promptly falling into an exhausted sleep.

CHAPTER TWO

THE next week flew by. Robbie responded to the medication and began sleeping better at night, allowing Jenna to catch up on her much-needed rest. Before she knew it, Mr Farnsworth and his secretary had departed, leaving her installed in the wide, plush executive office, waiting for the imminent arrival of her new boss.

She had put on her best suit, a rarely worn navy blue that she kept for special occasions. The skirt was pencil-slim and the blazer neat and businesslike. Her only concession to blatant femininity was a filmy, high-necked white lace blouse that made her feel fragile and helpless. Her hair was drawn back in a no-nonsense knot at the top of her head, but several long brown wisps were beginning to unravel and she knew she wouldn't have time to step into the washroom and spray them with hairspray to make them behave. Oh well, she sighed, Meg was the beauty of the family.

'Is staring out the window a normal part of your morning routine, Miss——?'

Jenna jerked around and stiffened under the piercing stare of her new employer.

'You!' Royce Drummond's face was a study in astonishment. The pupils of his eyes dilated so much that only tiny silver rings at the edges were visible. He stood tall and still in the doorway, facing her squarely, his dark trenchcoat slung over one shoulder and his briefcase in his other hand. '*You're* the paragon I was told about?' he demanded with shocked disbelief.

'I was asked to be your secretary, Mr Drummond. If you want someone else, I'll be happy to leave.' She stood quite still and waited for him to dismiss her, hoping she could maintain an air of cool confidence while making a dignified exit.

Deep down she knew it wouldn't work out. All her niggling doubts became more intense now as she looked at him standing here in front of her, his unconscious arrogance charging the very air between them. She had thought she could be so controlled, so detached, so very much in command. I knew better, but I had to try it, she berated herself.

His sudden laugh was loud, jarring and entirely without mirth. 'You were handpicked from the entire staff. Far be it from me to dispute Albert Farnsworth's choice of woman. Come to my office, Mrs Paragon.'

'The name is *Miss* Jennifer Caldwell, sir, or just plain Jenna.'

One thick black eyebrow quirked. 'Surely it's Mrs?'

'I'm not married.' As she lifted her chin, her face was cold and hard and full of dignity, her eyes sparkling blue fire as she challenged him with a look.

His eyes raked her body mercilessly. 'Are you so liberated it doesn't bother you to flaunt the fact that you're an unmarried mother?'

In spite of his insolent scrutiny, she dredged up an amazing poise. 'No, sir, I don't flaunt anything. No one here knows anything about my private life. You're the only one who knows I have a son, aside from my sister. It if becomes a source of gossip for the office, I'll know exactly where it started and I'll be forced to leave.'

'Heaven forbid that I be the one to drag you off your pedestal, Paragon. Your secret's safe with me.' His lips twisted as he stepped to his office and hung his coat on a walnut coat tree. Then he sat behind his desk and flicked open his briefcase, getting down to business. 'I want you to call a meeting of all the department heads for ten o'clock this morning and I want a detailed financial report of all expenditures for the last quarter. It's to be an informal meeting, but I want you there to take notes. Any questions?'

'Only one, sir.' She looked at him steadily, trying to remain unruffled by his brusque manner as he impatiently riffled through his desk drawers. 'About your phone calls.'

A grimace crossed his face. 'I suppose there've been some already?'

'Yes, sir. A Margo St John called three times and an Eva Travers twice.'

He leaned back in his chair with a trace of negligent amusement, studying the vivid stain of red creeping into her cheeks. 'What did they have to say? From the looks of you, it must have been good.'

'It was difficult to convince Miss St John that you weren't trying to avoid her. She gave me a detailed account of her prowess in bed and asked if I thought it was enough to keep you interested in her.'

He chuckled softly. 'And what did you say?'

'That I had no idea what you preferred and I would return her call when you got in. Shall I get her on the line for you now?' Jenna knew she was red with embarrassment and it galled her that she couldn't keep her face as expressionless as her voice.

His laugh was short before he raked an impatient hand through his hair and stared at her with his opaque, all-seeing eyes that held her and looked deep inside her.

She tried not to stare back, but she couldn't *not* look at him. He was the most handsome man she had ever seen. How could she have forgotten?

'Send Margo a dozen roses and make reservations for dinner at nine tonight at the Lighthouse,' he said so softly she shivered. 'Do the same for Eva Travers tomorrow.'

Jenna kept her face blank and wrote the names and times down on her pad. 'Do you have a preference as to the colour of roses, sir?'

'What colour are the ones I sent to Meg?'

'Red,' she all but choked, thinking of the way Meg had mooned over the full-blown buds that must have cost a fortune.

'Then make it yellow for Margo and white for Eva.'

She wrote it on her pad without a word. 'Is that all, sir?'

His lips twitched. 'Don't you approve?'

Her chin came up a fraction, but her voice was coolly calm and full of studied indifference. 'What you choose to do outside this office has nothing to do with me, sir. Just as my life has nothing to do with you. Is there anything else?'

'You've really perfected the put-down, haven't you?'

Somehow she kept her face blank, her body rigid, and didn't say a word.

'Call both women and tell them I'll pick them up shortly before the respective times. I don't have time to talk to either of them now,' he said irritably.

At his curt nod of dismissal, she walked with unhurried grace to her own office. When the heavy door closed softly behind her, she sagged back against it, shaking all over, her limbs protesting the taut way she had been holding herself. The only sound in the silent room was her own breathing, harsh and swift and shallow.

This was insanity—sheer, absolute insanity. She was way out of her league and she knew it. An unconscious charm oozed from every pore, and even as plain as she was, she was dangerously susceptible to it. If she let herself indulge in fruitless dreams it could only mean she'd spend the rest of her life with a broken heart, watching him go from one beautiful woman to another. She was a secretary, not a woman, to him. A shudder passed through her. All this past week it was Meg. Tonight, Margo St John. Tomorrow, Eva Travers. That should be enough to douse any romantic inclinations hidden in her heart.

I won't think about him that way, she told herself, pressing a shaking hand across her eyes. I'll be blind and deaf to everything that doesn't concern this office. Her fingers shook as she sat at her desk and reached for the telephone. In that moment she resolved to become the perfect secretary. She hadn't asked for any of this, but she was determined to make the most of what had been handed to her.

Every day became more of a challenge, and after nearly a month had passed, Jenna was desperately debating with herself whether or not to hand in her resignation. No, throw it at him was a better phrase. She wanted to shout, to rant and rave and scream at him for his inconsideration, not just to her but to everyone who worked for him.

Each morning she steeled herself to face his arrogant demand for perfection, but by the end of the working day, she was worn to a frazzle from trying to maintain a cool, poised façade of complete control and quiet acceptance of his commands.

He was inhuman, and he treated everyone else as if they, too, were machines incapable of human error. The hours he kept were irregular. There were days when he didn't come in at all. Whether he purposely didn't tell her where he was or when he'd be expected back was a question Jenna couldn't begin to find an answer for. And then there were days when he spent the whole of forty-eight hours in his office, taking it for granted that she would see his meals were sent in to him.

It seemed to her that he took a perverse delight in pushing everyone to the limit of his ability. And it wasn't only the corporate executives in the company who felt the sting of his merciless manipulations. The lowly stock boys and typists also knew when he was in the building.

But in just that short month, the agency had taken on a new look. People were beginning to notice them, and as a result, business was thriving.

'Miss Paragon!'

She jumped and her bemused glance found Royce Drummond standing stiffly, tight-lipped, glowering at her from the doorway connecting his office to hers. The morning sunlight slanted across the pale grey carpeting in bright rays, settling on the harsh lines of his haughty face.

'I want you to call maintenance and have them move your desk to the other side of the room. Now. Do you understand?'

The desk in question was small and neatly kept with a space for her typewriter on a pull out shelf at the side. It was placed at the end of the wide room with two large windows overlooking downtown Toronto behind it.

Bewilderment flickered across her face as she squared her shoulders in her stiffly starched white blouse. 'What's wrong with it right here, sir?'

'Everything's wrong with it,' he said with biting impatience. 'I will not tolerate you staring out windows when you're supposed to be working.'

Her mouth thinned and she sat up straighter as her temper flared. Somehow she managed, barely, to keep it under control. 'Mr Drummond, I am not neglecting my work. If you must know, the view from these windows helps me keep my equilibrium. When things get too—hectic—just looking at the skyline helps to put everything back into perspective.'

'This job's too much for you? Is that what you're saying?'

'Are you asking for my resignation?' she flared, secretly relieved that the decision was being taken out of her hands.

There was a menacing quality to his swift approach, and Jenna forced herself to sit absolutely still as he leaned across her desk, pinning her with his blazing grey eyes only an inch away from hers. 'You'd like to give it to me, wouldn't you?' he said softly through gritted teeth. 'You'd like to shove it down my throat.'

She was conscious of the taut hard angle of his jaw so close to her face, the straight chiselled nose with the flaring nostrils, the deep silver sheen of his eyes boring holes through her. 'Only if I could douse it with acid first!' she said just as softly.

Royce Drummond jerked his head back, blinking. Then she watched in fascination as the slashing grooves bracketing the sides of his face deepened into a grin. His laugh was deep and disconcerting as his anger hadn't been. 'I'm sure you'd enjoy that, but you were chosen for me, my paragon, and I can't take the time now to try to find a replacement for you. All right. Keep the desk where it is, if it amuses you. But I expect the work to be done.' He rubbed the back of his neck with an impatient hand. 'I need the Borchini file. Do you have it?'

She sifted through the small pile of folders on her desk and handed it to him without a word.

'Be ready to go to lunch at twelve instead of one today,' he said absently, already forgetting her as he flipped through the file and made his way back to his office.

Her hands curled into small impotent fists, but she didn't say a word. This was too much! Now he was dictating the time she called her own. It wasn't fair. Her temper seethed as she turned to stare out the window again, seeking comfort in the sight of the glass and steel crescent-shaped buildings standing serenely in the sunshine.

When she calmed down, she managed to find a plausible excuse for him. He probably had some important meeting scheduled during her usual lunch time. The trouble was, he never told her what he had in mind. She always had to second guess him, and it was becoming increasingly irritating. He might call her paragon, but she was merely human like everybody else, and she would appreciate a little consideration from him.

Maybe if I let myself go just once, she thought. Maybe if I vented my frustration and threw something or cried or . . . She sighed dejectedly and hunched over her typewriter. No, she couldn't be that way. She was just a secretary paid to do a job. She'd leave the dramatics to Meg.

Precisely at twelve, Royce Drummond emerged from his office looking as if he had just stepped out of an advertisement for some expensive men's clothing store. Jenna glanced at him but kept typing, not letting herself think about the handsomeness of this gorgeous man in his tailor-made black suit, white silk shirt and muted blue-grey tie. An unconscious sigh escaped her as she tried to focus her eyes on the letter in her typewriter. He might be a tyrant, but he was the most attractive one she'd ever seen! No wonder women were falling all over themselves wanting to go out with him.

If only I wasn't plain, she thought. If I'd been born beautiful like Meg, I might be going out to lunch with a man like him. I might . . .

'I don't like to be kept waiting, Miss Paragon.'

Her fingers jammed the keys and she looked up uncomprehendingly. She thought he'd already gone.

'I told you to be ready at twelve.'

Her face flushed guiltily. 'I didn't realise you wanted the office empty at this time.'

'What?'

'I intended to have a sandwich at my desk this afternoon. Er—they're repairing the sidewalk in the park where I usually go, so I thought I'd stay in. But if you'd rather I left——'

'I asked you to have lunch with me this afternoon.'

Her jaw dropped and she stared at him in stupefaction.

'I distinctly remember asking you to be ready at twelve.'

Jenna pulled herself together with difficulty. 'Asking me? You told me to be ready to take my lunch hour at twelve today instead of one o'clock.'

'Good God, does every man who asks you to lunch have to go through this?'

'Why would you want to take me?'

A very loud, very succinct epithet assaulted her ears before he ripped her coat off a hanger and threw it at her. 'Believe me, it's strictly business, in case you're letting your imagination run away with you. You can rest assured, I wouldn't dream of taking advantage of your hidden charms. Icebergs aren't my type.'

The insult made her shrivel with hurt. Somehow she thought he'd be above listening to petty office gossip.

'We're meeting some representatives of the

Borchini Company and I want you along to take some mental notes in case I miss something,' he said through his teeth.

'Oh.'

She felt very small as she preceded him out the door. The feeling persisted when she felt herself becoming the cynosure of all the eyes of her former co-workers as they walked through the halls, and it became magnified when she emerged from a taxi in front of an exclusive little restaurant in the heart of the city. The building itself didn't carry a name. There was just a small gold number on the grey brick.

'Now what?' Royce asked irritably as she shrank back toward the street, her hands hopelessly trying to restore order to the wind-tangled wisps of hair falling in her eyes.

'I—I'm not dressed for such a place.'

His sweeping gaze mentally stripped away her shapeless brown coat. 'You're wearing a dark skirt and some kind of white blouse. The sensible shoes are the only thing out of place. And this.' He reached up and roughly pulled the pins from the thick shiny knot on top of her head. 'Why you try to wear it up is beyond me.'

Her hair fell about her shoulders in untidy waves and she raked her fingers through it to keep it out of her eyes. 'It's a mess like this.'

'It's got great possibilities. Leave it.'

She didn't have time to argue with him. He gripped her elbow with punishing fingers and unceremoniously forced her into the restaurant.

The light was dim after the bright sunlight outside and she had trouble focussing, but the firm hand on her elbow kept her from tripping as her feet sank in the thick carpeting in the darkness. When her eyes became accustomed to the lack of lighting, she saw quite a few people seated at cosy round tables. At the far end of the room, three men rose courteously at their approach.

'Ah, Royce,' a dark wizened man with white hair greeted him.

'Mr Borchini,' he nodded, shaking his hand. 'I'd like you to meet my secretary, Jennifer Caldwell.'

'How do you do, Mr Borchini.' She felt him take her hand and kiss it gallantly, but her mind was falling all over itself. Royce Drummond actually knew her name! He'd never called her anything but 'Miss Paragon' for a month, and to hear him say it now unnerved her.

'Jennifer Caldwell?' Arturo Borchini inspected her thoroughly and frowned. 'Are you related to Margaret Caldwell?'

'I have a sister Margaret,' she said softly, looking to her employer for help, but he was shaking hands with the other two men on the table.

'My sons and my assistants, Carlo and Nicolo,' Mr Borchini gestured to them, finishing the introductions before stepping aside to let the tall blonde girl coming back from the ladies' room join them.

'Meg!' Jenna gasped.

'Jenna!' Her sister was just as shocked. 'What are you doing here?'

'I'm working,' she choked. It was on the tip of her tongue to ask where Robbie was and who was caring for him at this time of day and how many other times had Meg gone out to lunch like this. But she realised she couldn't say anything. She was still on the job. The only reason she was here was because she was a secretary, who had to keep alert and take mental notes. She couldn't let her own troubles intrude on her workday. This might be a social outing for Meg, but it wasn't for her. Using all her willpower, she forced her mind to concentrate on the job she was being paid to do.

Royce Drummond was holding a chair for her, frowning darkly at her preoccupation, and with a hurried gulp she sat down next to him. Meg was already seated across from them with the two handsome Borchini sons on either side of her. They smiled politely when they were introduced to Jenna, but it was obvious to everyone that they couldn't keep their eyes off Meg.

'Royce, I'm beginning to see how right you are,' Mr Borchini grinned widely, clapping him on the shoulder. 'Margaret is perfect. Her bone structure is striking. The eyes, the face, everything about her is perfection. Right, Carlo? Nicky?'

They immediately nodded their assent, and Jenna wondered if they realised what fools they were making of themselves.

Meg was dressed in a softly draped dress of sky blue wool that clung to her willowy figure like a gentle caress. Her hair had been done by a professional that morning, Jenna realised, looking at the smooth gold chignon at the nape of her swanlike neck. But she quickly put it out of her mind, because all she could do was wonder where she had left Robbie while she was having it done.

By the time a vintage wine was brought to

them and their meal was ordered, Jenna had successfully managed to hide her distress behind a calm face. From time to time she felt her employer turn from a lingering study of Meg to flick his burning eyes over her own features.

Flushing hotly, she barely controlled the mad impulse to smack his face. It was obvious he was comparing her to Meg, and in a case like that, she came out a loser every time. Meg was tall and voluptuous; Jenna was short and thin. Meg knew how to use make-up, but the only thing Jenna ever wore was a rose-coloured lipstick.

Royce Drummond might have been able to conceal his thoughts behind a bland impersonal mask, but the Borchini men were not so subtle, and Jenna dwindled in her chair, feeling more and more out of place.

'It's so hard to believe you're sisters,' Carlo kept saying. 'Meg is so beaut——'

His father nudged him sharply in the ribs. 'I'm sure your talents lie in other directions, Miss Caldwell,' he said in an attempt to smooth over his son's cutting blunder. 'It's not always the apparent beauty of a woman that is the most satisfying thing in the long run. Many plain women have been the moving force behind great success.'

'I understand what you're trying to say, Mr Borchini. I also understand why you need a beautiful model like Meg to help sell your cosmetics,' Jenna said softly, the sweep of her lashes concealing the hurt in her eyes. It twisted in her stomach and with an effort she smiled and tried to keep the stiffness out of her voice. 'Plain women like me can look at the ads and, if they're presented right, feel that by using your products, we, too, can look beautiful.'

Mr Borchini pursed his lips. 'Do you really believe that?'

'Of course.'

'I disagree,' Carlo said shortly. 'If there is no beauty to begin with, no one can believe using our products will create it.'

He might have been speaking in the abstract, but Jenna took it personally. Her face flamed at his cutting cruelty.

'Oh, come now! You must realise beauty is an illusion,' Royce Drummond cut in, becoming animated now that they were starting to talk business instead of staring at Meg. 'We're in the business of creating that illusion,' he said firmly. 'Now here's what we propose to do . . .'

Jenna felt the curling sensation of hurt expanding in her stomach as all the talk of beauty and cosmetics and the elusive images of advertising began floating around her. She was far removed from the world of beautiful women and every one of the men sitting here knew it. Still, she had to listen to it all.

An elegant meal was served by soft-footed waiters, and she watched while they ate with enthusiasm as they talked, but she could hardly eat a thing. Meg was asked for her opinion time and time again, with Carlo and Nicky hanging on her every word. But Jenna remained aloof, listening to the business discussed while trying to be as unobtrusive as possible.

She needn't have worried that they would notice her. When the plates had been cleared and the deal concluded with handshakes, she excused herself to go to the ladies' room and not one of the men took his eyes off Meg to acknowledge it.

Just once, she said to her unhappy reflection in the powder room mirror, just once to have a man look at me like they're looking at Meg ... She plunged her hands into ice cold water and splashed some in her face. Not since she was nineteen had she indulged in such jealous self-pity. There was no sense letting it get the better of her now. It wasn't worth the aggravation. Besides, she knew Meg must have just as much trouble coping with her flawless beauty as she did with her plainness.

The thought cheered her, and when she returned to the table, the Borchini men made a gallant departure and Royce Drummond turned to Meg. 'I'll drop your sister at the office, then take you home, all right?'

Meg smiled brightly, ignoring Jenna's silent signals to refuse. 'Of course, Royce. Anything you say. I'm so grateful to you for what you've done for my career. I'll be working with the best in the business now. Maybe on the way home you'll think of a way I can show my appreciation?'

Jenna's lips pressed into a tight thin line as she quickly slipped on her coat and turned away, trying not to picture all the other women in his life and the various ways they expressed their appreciation. Oh, Meg! I could shake you till your teeth rattle! Don't you see how depraved he is? And what about Robbie? The silent thought was stifled in her throat, but it ached all the same.

Thinking fast, she forced the censure out of her voice and gave both of them an innocent smile.

'Have you forgotten you were going to meet me after work today, Meg? This morning you said you had some shopping to do and then we'd go home together. I was looking forward to it.' She glanced at the narrow watch on her wrist. 'Goodness! It's three-thirty already. That doesn't give you much time, does it?'

The frosty glint of grey flashing from Royce Drummond's eyes told her she hadn't fooled him.

Meg stamped her foot in frustration, but he was not to be outdone.

'It's all right, Meg. I wouldn't want to interfere with your sister's plans this afternoon. How about dinner tonight? Shall I pick you up at eight?'

Meg's ill temper evaporated like mist in sunshine. 'I'll be ready.'

Sickened, Jenna turned away without another word.

But when she got home that evening, she let Meg feel the full force of her temper. 'I expected you to meet me after work!' she snapped.

'You just made that up so I couldn't spend the rest of the afternoon with Royce. All you ever do is window-shop anyway. You never spend any money. I needed the time to get ready for tonight.'

'What do you think you're doing,' Jenna exploded. 'All right, you want to model again—I can understand that. But to agree to work hand in glove with Royce Drummond is insanity. If you won't think of Robbie, think of me. I'm trying to provide for us. I want us to stay together as a family. Since Mom and Dad died, we're all we have left.'

'You've got a nerve, telling me not to work with him!' Meg rounded on her. 'You're his secretary! For somebody who doesn't want to get involved with him, you're not doing so well yourself! I was shocked when he told me you've worked together for a month already.'

'I'm not involved with him. I only see him in the office. I don't see him socially the way you do.'

'You looked pretty social to me this afternoon.'

Jenna let out a harsh breath and kicked off her shoes. 'That was the first time, and it was strictly business.'

'Some business,' Meg said spitefully. 'A three-and-a-half-hour lunch with the most handsome man in Toronto. Yet you won't even let me bring him home for a drink!'

'You *can't* bring him home. What about Robbie?'

'What about him?' Meg hissed. 'He knows you have a son. He wouldn't think anything of it.'

'Royce Drummond isn't stupid,' Jenna reminded her.

'That kid is ruining my life,' she wailed. 'I can't even bring a man home in the afternoon for a drink!'

'It wouldn't have been only a drink and you know it!'

Meg's face turned an ugly red. 'Since when have you started judging my morals? Robbie was an accident—I explained that. Peter was consoling me after Mom and Dad's funeral, but in ordinary circumstances it never would have happened.'

'You don't have to make excuses,' Jenna sighed, immediately apologising. 'I'm sorry I said anything. It's over and done with. I'm not judging you, I'm just trying to keep you from making another mistake.'

'Well, I'm not going to quit living. As soon as I start getting a salary, I'm finding somewhere else to live. I'm a big girl now and I can take care of myself,' declared Meg.

Meg would never know how much those words hurt. Her mother had made her promise to take care of Meg before she died, but Jenna had really botched the job. Failure and guilt, however unjustified, weighed heavily on her and she rubbed her temples with her fingers. 'Do we have any aspirin left? I've got a pounding headache.'

'In the bathroom,' said Meg with a pout. 'And be quiet, for heaven's sake! The kid's only been asleep for an hour. Mrs Graham watched him today and she said he was a regular little tartar, whatever that means.'

'I've asked you not to call him the "kid",' snapped Jenna, rapidly losing the tight control she kept on her emotions. 'And Mrs Graham's wrong. He's not bad-tempered, he's just recovering from a bad bout of bronchitis.' She sighed defeatedly. 'If you're going to be working now, we've got to find a more reliable babysitter. Someone younger, with more patience.' She shook the aspirins into her hand and walked back to the kitchen.

'Mrs Graham's good enough,' said Meg. 'With five of her own, she's got the experience, even if she doesn't have the patience.'

'No,' Jenna swallowed the aspirins with a grimace. 'Robbie needs a lot of love and attention. She won't do at all.'

'Oh well, you'll think of something,' Meg said brightly. 'After all, he's your son and your responsibility. I think that's Royce now.' She threw an exotic green satin cape over her shoulders and disappeared out the door.

CHAPTER THREE

JENNA leaned back in her chair and swivelled it to look out the window, seeking the calming influence of Toronto's skyline. All day, beautiful women paraded through her office to be interviewed by her boss for a new line of summer sportswear he had agreed to advertise. Having to maintain an air of cool unconcern and brisk efficiency in the face of such unequalled beauty left her drained. Her hair had long since come undone from its tidy knot and fell down her back in tangled brown waves. Finding a rubber band in the back of a drawer, she looped it around the hair at her nape and decided not to worry about it. The day was almost over anyway.

When Royce Drummond's office door opened, Jenna turned back to her desk, ready in case he barked out a command. But he didn't even see her. He only had eyes for the redhaired beauty clinging to his side.

She couldn't tear her gaze away from his bent head as he kissed the woman passionately on her moist red mouth. A shudder ran through her when she noticed the way she was pressing herself against the entire length of his body to make closer contact. Never in her wildest dreams could Jenna imagine being kissed like that.

There was a lot of heavy breathing before Royce seemed to remember where he was. He caught sight of Jenna and laughed at the colour running up her neck. 'We're embarrassing my secretary, Alexandra,' he said with a mocking grin. 'Perhaps we should continue this interview tonight in a more private place?'

'Oh, darling! That would be wonderful.' Her voice was husky and deeply sensuous. 'What time?'

'Will eight be all right?'

'That's per——'

'I'm sorry, sir,' Jenna cut in with an ice-cold voice, more angry at herself than at him. Why would she even want to picture herself in his arms? 'Have you forgotten you have a meeting tonight at seven? It'll take up most of the evening.'

'Meeting?' He stared at her blankly, trying to read her closed face.

'It has to do with transporting, sir.' A frown creased his forehead and she knew he didn't know what she was talking about. Maybe she should have worded it differently, but she couldn't baldly say he had a previous date, so she tried to make it sound like a business meeting. 'It came up suddenly last week, but you said you'd be there and I should remind you.'

'Oh, Royce,' the beautiful Alexandra pouted, 'can't you put it off?'

He continued to look at Jenna's set face, a resentful muscle quivering in his jaw, then he let out a small exasperated sigh. 'Am I free tomorrow?'

She consulted her calendar. 'Yes, sir.'

'Then how about tomorrow, Alexandra?' He turned on his most placating smile full of unspoken promise. 'Will I be worth the wait?'

Jenna turned away, sickened at all the phoney charm oozing from him, and made a pretence of looking for something in her bottom drawer. Her skin crawled when she heard the two of them murmuring throaty whispers.

If only I wasn't plain ... The refrain began again in her head and she forced it to stop. Even if she was beautiful, Royce Drummond wouldn't give her a second glance. She was his secretary, nothing more, and she was determined never to give him an inkling of how she was attracted to him. There was no way she'd leave herself open to the pain and unhappiness that would be sure to follow if she did. She could just imagine the laugh he'd have at her expense!

A short ragged breath caught in her throat when she noticed two highly polished black shoes standing close to her chair.

'Now what the hell do you mean, I have a meeting tonight?' he ground through his teeth, anger vibrating all around him.

Jenna straightened, trying to remain unruffled, and saw that they were alone. 'You offered to help Meg move to her new apartment,' she said quietly, getting to her feet and putting a safe distance between them.

'Does it have to be tonight?'

'You've put her off twice already, but you promised her nothing would stand in your way a third time. I realise you're beginning to lose interest in her, but she anxious to get settled in. And you did offer.'

He stared hard at her and finally let out a harsh breath. There was no way he could get out of it, but his anger had to find an outlet somewhere.

'Why couldn't she be like you?' he sneered. 'Being the efficient paragon that you are, you didn't have to ask for my help. You've already moved all your own things, and your son's, haven't you?'

She stiffened and lost a little of her colour. 'You offered to help Meg, Mr Drummond.'

'Does it make you feel high-and-mighty not to need anybody?'

She didn't answer him.

'Or do you need my help too, but you're just too proud to ask?' His tone took on a silky menacing quality and his eyes skimmed over her stiffly lifted chin.

'No, sir. I don't need your help.'

'Why not?'

She stared out the window.

'You aren't going with Meg,' he said slowly, tilting his head to one side, searching her closed expression. 'You aren't, are you? I can tell by the way you've clammed up.'

'It has nothing to do with you.'

'So where are you going if not with her?'

Jenna pressed her lips tightly together, not answering.

'Meg told me the house you're living in has been sold and the new owners have given you only a month's notice to find other living quarters. That was two weeks ago. Have you found something? Have you already moved out?'

Her breath was expelled harshly, letting him know without saying anything she found his questioning offensive.

But he didn't take the hint. 'It can't be easy, finding a place that allows children. Meg left you in the lurch, didn't she? I know she's not too fond of dirty diapers and spilled milk, from the things she'd said.'

'I've told you before, my private life is private. Where I live and with whom has nothing to do with you.'

'If you need a bigger salary to afford a decent place for your son, all you have to do is ask.'

Her chin shot up and her lips tightened to a thin white line. Her rigid pride would ask nothing from him for Robbie. 'That's not at all necessary. My salary is more than adequate. It's my problem. I'll handle it in my own way. I told Meg to expect you at seven.' She turned back to her desk, but he stepped in front of her, blocking her way, his whole manner relentlessly probing.

'Not so fast! I've gone and done it, haven't I?'

Jenna shivered, averting her face at the sudden gentling of his tone, trying to ignore the trickle of nervousness slithering down her spine. 'I don't know what you mean.'

'Yes, you do. Whenever I mention anything about your son, I can see a change come over you. There's hurt in your eyes even though you try to hide it behind that wall of ice. Did you love his father very much?'

She jerked away violently, glaring at him, contempt in every trembling limb. 'You have no right to ask me such a thing!' The grim twisting of his lips goaded her on. 'You don't know what love is. You, of all people, have no right to even mention that word!'

It was only a heart-stopping instant before his long arms reached for her, crushing her shoulders, pulling her close to the rigid length of his body.

'Why? Why do you say me—of all people? You know women fall all over me. They tell me I'm a great lover.' He was shaking with rage, his fingers becoming tight iron talons.

'What you feel isn't love,' she choked, struggling, trying to twist away from him.

His fingers ripped the rubber band from her hair before threading through the tangled brown thickness. 'You know all about it, don't you?' he muttered close to her face. 'You with your disdainful little smiles and carefully blank expressions. You're always judging me, aren't you? You, a woman who was dragged off her pedestal a long time ago. Every time you see me with a woman you despise me for taking what she offers. Or is it yourself you despise?'

Jenna thought she had perfected the mask of indifference, but it was suddenly shattered, exposing all her fruitless yearning to his eyes. Oh, how could she? She should have known she couldn't handle the attraction he had for her. She should have avoided him like the plague. Where was all the cool disdain that helped her through these last two months?

Her breath was strangling in her throat and she fought against the mad pounding of her heart and the tremors racing up and down her spine. 'Let me go,' she breathed, trying to dredge up the ice-cold voice always so effective in keeping men away before.

Royce searched her shimmering blue eyes so bright with repudiation, and his voice shook. 'Did he promise you the world, then walk out on you? Is that what's turned you into this frigid little iceberg?'

Her eyes closed. At once she wished she'd kept them open. She could feel the violence in him, the taut power of his legs pressed against hers making her traitorous body tremble, and the bruising pressure of his hands in her hair, holding her still, arching her neck up to him.

This never should have happened, she thought wildly. I never should have said anything. I should have let him go with that last model and hired someone to help Meg.

Trying to despise him, she was shocked at this boneless, floating loss of control over her own body. She struggled against the sensation, hating herself, knowing it was madness.

'You must have loved a man once,' he murmured huskily. 'Is there any of the passion you must have felt left? Or has all that ice choked out the fire?' His lips brushed the curve of her neck as she arched away from him, tasting the warm creamy skin, feathering along her madly pounding pulse before making his way to her mouth, where he surprised her by gently resting his lips against hers before brushing them back and forth in a caress.

She expected him to be ruthless and demanding. But when he wasn't, somewhere deep inside her an unsuspected sensation flared, trapping her in its gripping spell. Shaking, she found herself clinging to him, her hands mindlessly curling into the bunching muscles of his back and shoulders. She was stunned by this instinctive response, maddened by its all-enveloping power.

He wasn't content with tasting her lips for long. He gently coaxed them apart, insistent, relentless, tantalising.

Shocked at this violation of her senses, and her own trembling delight in it, Jenna shuddered, hating herself more and more but powerless to move away from him.

'Mmmm, you taste good,' he murmured into her mouth. 'And the scent of your skin fills my mind. What kind of perfume are you wearing? I don't recognise it.'

Jenna's whole body clenched with a violent stiffening jerk. She never wore perfume but Robbie's baby powder always seemed to cling to her skin and everything she wore. Robbie! And here she was in the arms of the one man who must never know of his true parentage.

Wrenching herself away from him, she breathed deeply, trying not to let him see how much he affected her.

He didn't move. His arms hung lifelessly at his sides. His face was as white as hers was red, his eyes a brilliant opaque grey, watching all kinds of turbulent emotions chasing across her face before she could capture them and hide them behind an indifferent mask.

'Well, well,' he said unsteadily.

'If you're through amusing yourself, Mr Drummond, I'll be going. It's after five.' Her voice could have frozen the warmest summer sun. It must give him some kind of thrill to go from one woman straight into the arms of another. Surprisingly her legs didn't buckle when she stepped past him to her desk. Of all the idiotic things she had ever done in her life, this was the worst. Why don't I take a number and stand in line along with all the other women blinded by his charm? she thought wretchedly, whipping up an anger to wipe out all the other traitorous emotions swamping her. I wonder what colour roses he'd choose for me? She wanted to laugh. The thought of this gorgeous man kissing a girl like her was ludicrous. It only proved no one was immune to the charm of depravity. She should have had more sense.

His mouth thinned as, apparently unmoved, she gathered her things together in silence. 'What, no hysterics? No, "you'll have my resignation on your desk first thing in the morning"?'

Jenna kept her voice low. 'If that's what's happened to every other secretary you've ever had, I'm afraid you're going to be disappointed this time. I need this job more than I despise you. Would you have me resign because you gave in to a sudden mad impulse?' Her chin lifted with all that was left of her tattered pride. 'Alexandra is a very beautiful woman and you wanted her. I realise I made you angry when I reminded you of your promise to Meg. You were merely venting your frustration on me.'

'Is that right?' he sneered, looking suddenly wounded. 'And do you consider it one of your duties as the paragon of secretaries to respond the way you did to a mere "venting of frustration?"'

It was all she could do to force an answer through her stiff lips. 'You don't need me to tell you you're an expert in the art of seduction. You probably could wring a response from a stone!'

'But it didn't really touch you? Is that what you're saying?'

'I'm sorry if I'm bruising your ego, but no, you didn't really touch me.'

'Your body told me differently.'

'My body, perhaps. But my soul, no.'

His face became livid. 'You don't have a soul, Paragon!'

Jenna gave him a cold little smile full of as much disdain as she could find and started out of the office.

'I'll take you home,' Royce muttered ungraciously. 'Since you made sure I'd have to go your way anyway.'

'No, thanks.' She didn't even turn around. 'I'm not going home yet.'

'Do you mean you actually have a date?' he sneered. 'Who's the lucky man? Don't tell me, let me guess. Chad Redwicke? I've noticed how much time he spends in the halls ogling all the girls. He's probably the type to make your cold little heart flutter.'

Not responding to the jibe, she quietly walked away.

The subway was fast and efficient even at this time of day with its rush-hour crowds on their way home. Somehow the noise and jostling bodies all around her put everything back into perspective. Nothing had happened really. She would forget it as quickly as possible. It meant nothing. Women were a game to men like Royce Drummond. They were there for him to pursue, to conquer, then discard. He probably saw her as a challenge. Her deliberately cool manner made him think she was immune to his charm, and he just couldn't resist finding out if it was true. Too bad, she smiled to herself; it had to be the first time he had failed, and that wouldn't put him in the best of moods for Meg tonight.

As the stations flitted by, she stared straight ahead, oblivious to everything, her mind busily planning her evening.

In a few more minutes she'd collect Robbie and take him to the zoo. She'd have a stand-up meal along the way and bide her time until it was safe to go back home. This is the last time, she promised herself. After tonight she'd never have to plan evenings like this again.

Meg was determined to leave and live her own life and couldn't be talked out of it, so, not really ignoring her responsibility, Jenna made herself look at it from a positive point of view. Meg was an adult now. She'd keep an eye on her, but it was time to let her stand on her own two feet. Besides, she was removing the ever-present threat of Royce Drummond discovering Robbie's relationship to him. Now that Meg had found another place to live, Jenna would be able to breathe easier in the evenings, knowing there was no possibility of him unexpectedly calling on Meg and seeing her son.

Watching her from the front window, Robbie gurgled contentedly in the arms of the tall smiling woman Jenna had found to babysit. Coming up the walk to the neat snug house, Jenna let her expression soften. Kate Malloy had been the answer to one of her prayers. Over tea with Mrs Gresham one evening, she had been introduced to this pretty woman who had been her neighbour before moving to the affluent suburb of Scarborough. Having no children of her own, she told Jenna she had been on a list, waiting to adopt, for the last three years. Now that she was twenty-eight, she was beginning to

worry that she was too old. When Jenna
mentioned that she needed someone to care for
Robbie, Kate had jumped at the chance, and now
they had a running, goodnatured argument as to
who benefited most from this arrangement. Kate
was crazy about Robbie, and Jenna was relieved
to be able to leave him in such good hands.

'I think we've finally got that bronchitis
licked,' said Kate, letting her into the cosy living
room where Robbie's toys were scattered all over
the floor. 'Hardly a wheeze out of him all day. All
that fresh air and sunshine's made a difference,
don't you think?' She was talking to Jenna but
grinning at Robbie, buttoning his little red jacket
and tilting his hat to a rakish angle.

'It couldn't be all that T.L.C. you give him,
could it?' Jenna smiled.

'Well, maybe I do give him a lot of tender
loving care.' Kate hugged him tightly. 'These
grey eyes of his are so big and beautiful. And this
dimple in his chin! When he grows up, he's going
to have women standing in line just waiting for a
glance from him.'

Jenna laughed. 'You're a riot! It's a good thing
he doesn't understand what you're saying, or he'd
be unbearably conceited.'

'But it's true—I swear. Can't you see how
gorgeous he's going to be?'

She could see it. More and more his looks
reminded her of another more forceful, darkly
handsome man. She wondered if Peter
Drummond looked like Royce, but she pushed
that thought away at once.

'I never knew you were such a romantic, Kate.
It must be all those books you read.' Her eyes

slid to the bookshelves crammed with paperbacks on a far wall.

'Maybe so. Don't you just love the thought of an innocent girl's love taming a desert shiek or brooding matador?' She pointed to a small stack on the table beside her. 'I just got this shipment today and I can't wait to start reading!'

Jenna shook her head. 'The women who write them ought to be shot for filling up women's heads with such nonsense.'

Kate's face fell. 'What have you got against romance? You know love is what makes the world go round.'

'And look at the state the world's in today,' Jenna said wryly.

'Love isn't the cause of the mess. Don't you see? It's because people aren't loving any more that we're in trouble. There's too little romance. Nobody trusts anybody. They're afraid of the commitment it requires. They don't want to get hurt, so they won't allow themselves to love.'

Jenna looked at her and sighed. I was that way not too long ago, she thought, ready to defend love and romance. 'It's simply a grand illusion,' she said bitterly. 'Fine for dreams and novels, but not for real life.'

'You sound so bitter,' she frowned, handing Robbie to her. 'Yet you must have loved somebody once——' She stopped. 'I'm sorry, Jenna, I sound like I'm prying. Forget what I said.'

'It's all right, Kate. I'm not bitter. I know love's out there somewhere waiting for me. I just won't let myself be blinded by it. Love tends to do that to people, you know.'

'Sometimes that's not a bad thing. There are times when it helps to be blind.'

Like when I see what a rat my boss is, Jenna thought with a cold twisted smile, suddenly feeling an intense rush of dislike for him welling up. All the women who loved him couldn't see past his good looks and charming manner and easy smiles. But she knew that underneath he never really returned their love. In the two months she'd worked for him, she felt she knew him inside out. Perhaps she knew him better than he knew himself. His was a fatal fascination.

When Royce Drummond came into his office the next morning, Jenna was already deep into the pile of correspondence on her desk, her feelings hidden under ice. She looked up with her polite secretary's smile when the door opened, and by some miracle, kept it glued to her face.

He looked as if he'd been up all night. The strong line of his jaw was dark with a day's growth of beard. His rich black hair stood on end. His tie was untied, hanging loose about his neck, the top few buttons of his shirt unbuttoned, his collar sticking out haphazardly over the lapel of his creased jacket.

His bloodshot eyes held hers for a long disturbing moment in the thick silence. 'You didn't come home last night,' he croaked. 'Where were you?'

Jenna's jaw started to drop, but she sank her teeth into her bottom lip, ignoring the loaded question. She turned back to her typewriter and began to hit the keys, but he reached out and stopped her.

'Please!'

'Do you have a headache, Mr Drummond?' It was a sarcastic jibe she couldn't resist. His hectic lifestyle was finally catching up with him. She wondered what Meg looked like.

'Where were you last night?' he demanded. 'I waited until three.'

She pretended not to hear. 'Would you like me to get you some aspirin? Or a cup of black coffee?'

The silver sheen of his eyes suddenly flared as they slid over her. 'Answer me!' He grabbed his head with both hands. 'What the hell did you have in that decanter?'

'Decanter?' She stiffened in shock and her eyes widened. 'The cut glass one in my kitchen?'

He tried to nod, but the movement obviously hurt his already aching head.

'Oh no!' Her face turned white as she stared at him. 'You didn't drink it!'

'What was it?' he groaned.

She put a clenched hand to her mouth and bit it hard. 'Last summer Meg and I bought a kit and tried to make some wine. Something went wrong with the fermentation process. It didn't turn out right, but I thought it was a pretty colour, so I kept it in the decanter. Nobody was supposed to drink it! You've probably been poisoned! Why didn't Meg stop you?'

'Meg wasn't there.' He shuddered and went to his own office, where he sagged on to a low leather sofa, groaning miserably.

Jenna followed him, wondering what she should do. 'Couldn't you tell just by smelling it that it was no good?'

'At first I thought it was some kind of liqueur. The first glass didn't taste too bad. So I made myself at home waiting for you.'

'The first glass? How much did you drink?'

'Three-quarters of what was there.'

She closed her eyes. 'I think you'd better get to a hospital.'

'No.' Royce leaned his head back and rubbed his hands over his face. 'Maybe if I just stay quiet for a while, I'll be all right. I have my paragon ... to ... take care ...'

'I'd feel better if you'd——' She stopped. He was already asleep.

Or was he unconscious? She took his wrist and felt for his pulse. It was weak but steady. Biting her lip, she put his arm down and rummaged through a small closet concealed in the panelled wall to find a blanket to cover him. His face was deathly white and there were blue circles under his eyes. Maybe he could sleep it off and be all right after he had rested. She removed his shoes and eased him out of his jacket before closing the curtains and quietly going back to her own office full of trepidation.

What if he died? She'd always feel it was her fault. Why didn't I throw that wine away? she berated herself. But how was I to know anybody would drink it? Maybe I should call a doctor and have him come here and examine him? She thought of the speculation and gossip that would spread through the building if she did and decided against it. I'll just have to take care of him myself, she thought. Her face was white and she groaned with self-reproach.

Somehow appointments were cancelled and

meetings re-scheduled. All through the day, between watching over Royce to make sure he was still breathing, Jenna fielded harassed queries from various department heads and dealt with the parade of beautiful women who just happened to drop in on the off chance that he'd be free.

A million glib excuses popped into her head and by going-home time she felt she had used them all. A day of such brisk efficiency left her drained.

All the offices were empty and dark when she looked in on him again. Flicking on a small lamp, she saw he was still on the sofa, but he had shifted his position and now his neck was oddly bent against the arm to an uncomfortable angle. She knew when he woke up he would not only have a headache but also a stiff neck.

It was long past leaving time and even though Kate had told her not to worry about being late to pick up Robbie, she began to panic. She couldn't leave Royce here like this all night, but she couldn't stay too much longer either. She was tired and irritable and wanted to get home. She and Robbie hadn't spent the most restful night last night in the motel after the taxi had driven by her house at midnight and found Royce's car still parked outside.

Ever so gently, she tried to shift his bulky body to ease the strain on his neck, but when she put her arms around his chest to lift him, he began to turn over and she was pulled down and trapped underneath him.

He opened one bleary eye and looked straight into her face. His arms were right around her, holding her close. 'You're real, my paragon,' he murmured thickly. 'I've dreamt of you so often.'

His heavy hands roamed over her body in the simple dress she wore, quivering along the slender curve of her hip.

Jenna dragged in a sharp quick breath. 'Wake up, Mr Drummond!'

He watched her lips move, fascinated. 'My name is Royce. Let me hear you say it.'

She gave a groan of dismay. This couldn't be happening to her. Now he was confusing her with one of his women.

'Say it!'

'Let me go, Royce,' she said coldly.

He blinked and shook his head in a daze. Time seemed to stop as they looked at each other in silence. Something flashed in his eyes, but it was gone so quickly she couldn't tell what it was. The vulnerable curve of his mouth softened.

He levered himself up on one arm. looking around blankly, letting her go before he struggled to a sitting position. 'What happened?' he muttered.

Relief ran through her with a rush. He hadn't been awake. What he said had been from some leftover dream. 'You've been asleep most of the day. How do you feel now?'

'Oh, I remember now. You tried to poison me.'

A guilty red ran into her face. 'I suppose in a way it was my fault. But nobody asked you to make yourself at home in my house and drink what was there.'

'I was waiting for you.' He dragged his hand through his hair. 'It was the only thing I could find in your cupboards.'

'Why were you waiting? Why didn't you just go home?'

He looked slightly taken aback, as if no woman had ever asked him that before. 'I wanted to apologise for what happened yesterday,' he muttered.

Jenna gritted her teeth. 'I've already forgotten it, Mr Drummond. It was an unfortunate lapse that I'm sure won't happen again.'

He stared at her. 'But it almost did happen again. Or did I dream it?' He shook his head and scrubbed his hands over his face before looking up at her. 'You felt so good in my arms, so right somehow, as if you belonged . . .'

A strangled gasp struck in her throat.

'Where were you anyway?'

'We went all through that before. Are you feeling better now?'

'I feel like I've been run over by a truck. What time is it?' He tried to focus on his watch, but couldn't see it.

'It's seven-thirty. If you're all right, I'll be going.' She started for the door, but he reached out and caught the hem of her dress.

'You haven't answered my question.'

'I told you it was seven-thirty.'

'I mean the question before that.' He swore softly. 'The question you're trying to ignore. Where were you last night? What time did you finally get home? Or didn't you get home at all?' His bleary eyes narrowed accusingly.

'What are you? Some irate father? I don't have to answer to you.' She was getting into deep water, and if she wasn't careful, she'd find herself floundering.

'I knew it! You didn't go home.'

She lifted her chin, her eyes meeting his

steadily. She couldn't do anything about the wild red colour sweeping into her face, but she could stop the questioning right now. 'Do you think you're the only one who has a wild private life? What I do or where I go or with whom I sleep has nothing to do with you. Now, if you'll excuse me, I'm late.'

His breath bubbled up harshly in his throat and he dragged his hands back over his face. 'Why do you do it, Paragon? You deliberately project an air of mystery.'

Jenna forced a wintry smile to her face. What he didn't know wouldn't hurt her. 'Goodnight, Mr Drummond.'

He looked better the next morning, more like himself again, but something indefinable had changed. When she sat waiting for him to begin his morning dictation, instead of starting as usual, he simply looked at her. She couldn't imagine what he was thinking, but her chest tightened so painfully it hurt to breathe. His silvery eyes slowly wandered over her and when he finally did begin, she hoped he wouldn't notice the way her pencil shook.

His voice was lilting and seductive and she had to keep telling herself to concentrate. This was a business letter. But her traitorous mind had a will of its own. She kept imagining that sensuous voice murmuring *I've dreamt of you so often* . . .

'Jennifer,' he murmured softly, holding a folder out to her.

It was a full minute before she realised he had stopped dictating and had been trying to get her attention. Her face flamed and she nervously jumped to her feet. When she took the folder from him, his fingers touched hers inadvertently and she drew back as if his touch would leave marks on her skin.

'That's all for this morning,' he said, his lips tightening. 'You may go.'

Trembling, Jenna made her way to her own office, calling herself all kinds of a fool.

Just as she sat down behind her desk, her office door opened and a teenaged, freckle-faced boy came in with a long florist's box tied with red ribbon.

'Flowers for Miss Jennifer Caldwell,' he said brightly, a wide smile playing about his generous mouth.

She looked at him and all at once became livid. 'Get them out of here!' she muttered through her teeth.

The smile was wiped right off his face. 'Do you mean you're refusing them?'

'That's exactly what I mean.' She stood behind her desk, her hands clenched at her sides, her face white with sudden rage.

'But—but I've never had this happen before. Please, miss, you've got to take them. What will I do with them?'

If he didn't get them out of here, she'd ram them down Royce Drummond's throat and probably lose her job. How dared he treat her as if she was one of his women!

'Take them home and give them to your mother—or your girl-friend—or dump them in the trash. I don't really care,' she said stiffly. 'I will not accept them.'

'But, miss——' he pushed back his cap and scratched his head, 'I've never had this happen before!'

She quickly signed his delivery book and then pushed the box at him. 'Take them home with you,' she grated. 'You won't be in any trouble. I'm giving them to you.'

'But don't you even want to see them first? They're beautiful. They're——'

'No! Just go!' She got a grip on herself and struggled to keep it. She wasn't interested in knowing what colour roses he might have chosen for her. He had a nerve, thinking she'd accept them. 'Please, just go!'

When the boy had left, muttering to himself, Jenna dragged her hands across her face and slumped into her swivel chair, turning to the windows. She needed the calming influence of the Toronto skyline more than ever now. Her stricken eyes sought the thin spiral of the C.N. Tower in the distance, soaring proudly above all the other buildings. It was the tallest free-standing structure in the world and she drew comfort just from looking at it.

I'll be like that tower, she thought, struggling to crush her churning emotions, all alone in the middle of a crowd. I've never wanted to lean on anybody before and I'm not going to let Royce Drummond near enough to try to wreck that independence now. How dare he!

When she turned back to her desk, she stiffened. Her employer stood in his doorway, tall and silent, a black scowl on his handsome face.

'Don't you ever do that to me again, Mr Drummond,' she said calmly, feeling a strange flicker of satisfaction curl in her stomach. 'I'm not one of your women, to be wooed with roses.'

'How do you know I sent them?' he asked

grimly, his lips white. 'And how do you know they were roses? And who the hell is wooing you?'

'It's the crass sort of thing you try with every woman,' she flung at him. 'I'm not like any one of them!'

'Ah yes, how could I forget? You're the paragon. Mere roses wouldn't do for you, would they? They're too common.' He stepped close to her desk and leaned across it, staring into her flashing eyes. 'What will it take to reach that cold little heart of yours barely beating under all that ice?'

'Haven't you heard?' Her voice dripped acid. 'Paragons aren't real. We don't have hearts.'

Royce straightened at once, almost as if she had struck him. And then he started to laugh, long and hard. 'I'll have to remember that!'

CHAPTER FOUR

IT was ten o'clock that evening before Jenna managed to relax. She had settled a restless and unusually irritable Robbie for the night and was immersed in the bathtub when her doorbell rang. Squeezing her eyes shut, she let out a harsh sigh. Why should she be surprised? Nothing had gone right yet today. Her first impulse was to ignore it, from the impatient sound of whoever kept his finger pressed down, she knew he wasn't going to give up and go away until he managed to wake up the baby.

'I'm coming—I'm coming,' she muttered hurriedly, barely drying off before pulling a fluffy white terrycloth robe around her. Her hair was damp around her face, long dark tendrils escaping from her topknot, and her skin was still flushed and rosy from the hot water as she ran across the living room. Standing behind and a little to one side of the door, she opened it a crack. Her eyes widened for a shocked instant before she reacted instinctively and started to slam it shut.

'Wait!' Royce said quickly.

'Meg isn't here. It's very late and I'm just about to go to bed.' Her voice was freezing.

He stepped closer and wedged his shoe between the door and the jamb. 'I didn't come to see Meg. I want to talk to you.'

'Can't it wait until tomorrow?'

'No, it's got to be now. Please let me in.'

It was too dangerous. 'I have a telephone, Mr Drummond. You didn't have to make a special trip over here.'

He glanced back over his shoulder. 'I'd rather not discuss this on the phone or on your doorstep. I won't stay long, I promise.'

The slight curving of his lips was meant to soften her up, she knew, but she remained immune. 'I'm not dressed for visitors,' she said irritably, noticing he looked impeccable in a dark sports coat and white turtleneck sweater.

'I've seen you in your robe before. Remember the night we first met?'

A miserable red ran into her face. She tried to close the door, but his foot blocked her efforts.

'Jennifer, please!'

It was useless to fight him and when she finally gave in, she would only look more a fool. Robbie was asleep. She'd probably be safe enough for a few minutes.

With a short sigh, she stepped back, opening the door to let him in. 'All right, Mr Drummond. Like the first time, you've got five minutes. What is it you wanted to discuss?'

He silently closed the door and stood just inside it, looking at her, skimming over her tousled hair and thick robe to her bare toes curling into the carpet. He kept one hand suspiciously behind his back. 'I want to start over. On the right foot this time.'

Her jaw started to drop. This was the last thing she expected him to say. Gripping her robe tightly in front of her, she frowned warily, but didn't trust herself to say anything.

'I've never met anyone like you before,' he went on softly. 'No matter how much I bully you, you're equal to it. You're fantastic in your work, and what's more, you catch things I miss and never say anything about them. You just correct them. I've come to realise what a goldmine I've got, and I want to keep you.' He took a square white box from behind him, holding it out to her with slightly shaking hands. 'I'd like you to accept this in the spirit it's intended.'

This definitely took the wind out of her sails. If he had been arrogant or cutting, she would have been able to handle him, but here he was, almost humble.

She tilted her head to one side and looked at him uneasily, trying to decide if it was all an act. He wasn't running true to form and she definitely didn't trust him. 'There's no need for this, Mr Drummond. You pay me a good salary and I enjoy the challenge of working as your secretary. You don't have to worry that I'll leave you.'

'But I do. No one else would have been able to cover for me while I passed out in my office and still have the business run as smoothly as if I'd been there myself. Oh yes,' he said quickly when she would have contradicted him, 'I heard from Redwicke in Graphics—about everybody who pestered you yesterday. I ought to get a revolving door . . . But nobody knew I was there. They all thought I was out tending to business. In just this short time I've come to rely on you. I owe you a lot. Please.' He forced the box into her hands.

Not trusting him for one minute, Jenna

blushed hotly. Then curiosity got the better of her and, opening the box, she drew in a sharp breath when she saw a small bunch of warm wet violets. A sudden swift rush of feeling ran through her. They weren't his awful roses! 'Mr Drummond——'

'Please don't refuse them. I hoped you'd like them. They remind me of you.'

She blinked suddenly wary eyes and watched as he turned on his heel and headed for the door.

'Goodnight, Jennifer,' he said softly.

'Goodnight, Mr——'

A harsh choking cough cut off his name. The sound of Robbie trying to cry and gasp for breath at the same time came from the bedroom.

'Is your son ill?' he asked, his hand on the doorknob.

'He's got bronchitis,' she said quickly. 'It flares up every once in a while.'

'Shouldn't you see to him?'

'Of course.' *But I have to get rid of you first*, she thought wildly, smiling, trying not to show her panic.

She nearly pushed him out the door and ran to the bedroom, still clutching the box of violets. Setting it down on a small table, she lifted Robbie in her arms and tried to soothe his harsh breathing. 'Don't panic, darling. You're all right.'

It took nearly fifteen minutes to quiet him, leaning him over a doubled-up pillow at his stomach and rubbing his back. When she finally had him breathing normally again, she laid him back in his cot—then stopped dead.

Royce Drummond was standing in the doorway watching her.

This is it, she thought, lifting her chin, clenching her jaw, waiting for the violent explosion of anger to follow his sudden recognition of his nephew.

But nothing happened.

She stood waiting, staring at him, but all he said was, 'Is he all right now?'

She nodded dumbly.

'I know you didn't want me to stay, but he sounded as if he was in trouble. I thought you might need my help—to take him to a hospital or something.' He came to stand beside the cot looking down at the baby. 'You scared your mother, didn't you?' he said softly, reaching out to ruffle the dark hair so like his own.

But still he didn't see the resemblance.

'Are you all right?' he asked, looking at Jenna's colourless face.

He didn't recognise his nephew! All this time she had worried for nothing. She looked down at Robbie, now drifting off to sleep, his breathing less laboured, and wanted to scream with relief.

'He really scared you, didn't he? Your face is so white now. All the time you worked on him you were so much in control. But now . . .' Royce put his arm around her shoulders and gently led her out of the room.

She didn't even think to protest.

'Come and sit down,' he murmured soothingly. 'I know you'd rather I didn't stay, but could I get you something?' He looked at a loss for a moment. 'What's called for in this situation? I know you haven't anything except that poison I had the other night.'

'Some good strong tea,' she whispered, staring

straight ahead with unseeing eyes. He didn't recognise Robbie! He had big grey eyes and black hair and a deep dimple in his chin, just like Royce himself, but he didn't recognise him. She tried to drag herself together. 'I'll get it. Er—would you like some? Or coffee?'

'Thank you. I'd like coffee, but I'll make it.'

'No, I'm all right, really.'

But he didn't listen to her. He'd already gone to the kitchen and she could hear him rummaging through her cupboards.

She couldn't believe her luck. If he had realised who Robbie was, he would have said something, given some indication. There had been nothing but sympathy in his warm grey eyes, compassion carved on his handsome face. Jenna's relief was so great she was able to pull herself together and lean back against the sofa and actually smile when he came back with two steaming cups and put them on the end table before sitting beside her.

'That's better,' he smiled. 'Your colour's coming back. Does this sort of thing happen to him often?'

She shook her head. 'It used to, but the attacks are less frequent now. I'm hoping he'll grow out of it.'

'That's good. I know my mother had quite a time with Peter when he was a baby. He had allergies. For a while there, the doctors thought it was asthma, but it just turned out he was allergic to all sorts of things. I suppose he told you?'

'No.' She busied herself with her teacup, hoping he wouldn't see the bright colour stealing into her face. 'Peter was more Meg's friend than mine. It was good of you to stay,' she said softly, searching desperately for something to change the subject. 'And I really do like the violets. How did you know I would?'

Royce grinned. 'You wouldn't even look at my roses, and even though you try to act the part of a very liberated lady, I knew underneath it all there had to lurk an old-fashioned girl. If you'd been as cold and heartless as you want everyone to believe, you wouldn't have gone to all the trouble of having that baby of yours. You'd have had an abortion and that would have been the end of it.'

Jenna choked softly. 'I couldn't let that happen.'

'I'm glad. He's a beautiful child.'

She pushed back the brown wisps of hair falling in her eyes and nervously licked her lips. Why couldn't they find something else to talk about? He might start putting two and two together. 'Er—have you seen Meg tonight? Does she like her new apartment? I wanted to ring her, but her phone hasn't been installed yet.' She knew she was babbling, but she had to change the subject.

He drained his cup and leaned across her to set it on the table. 'No, I haven't seen her.' He stayed in this bent position and looked directly into her burning face. 'You know, I never realised it before, but she's really empty-headed. Most of the women I know are like that. You're the only one who's different.'

Jenna pressed herself as far back into the sofa cushions as she possibly could. 'Since I wasn't blessed with a pretty face, Nature made up for it by giving me brains instead,' she explained.

'Who says you're not pretty?' His voice was husky and he leaned closer.

'Stop it right there, Mr Drummond,' she said icily, her face set in freezing fury. 'Just what are you leading up to?'

He stayed leaning over her but raised both hands, letting them hover near her shoulders. 'What makes you think I'm leading up to anything?'

'I know a line when I hear one. I'm not pretty, I'm plain. Let's not kid ourselves, shall we? You've given me flowers. You've poured on the charm. You're smiling and seductive. What comes next?'

'A proposal of marriage, what else?' he said coldly, stung. 'I want you to marry me, Jennifer.'

She stared at him for a long moment, searching his face. 'That does it!' She jumped to her feet, pushing at his chest to get him out of the way, then stood stiff and still, glaring at him. 'If you don't leave here this instant, I'll call the police and have them arrest you for harassment!'

His eyebrows rose in a thick black line over grim eyes. 'That's not quite the reaction I expected.'

'What am I suppose to do? Throw myself at you feet and grovel in thanksgiving because a man as handsome as you are has seen fit to notice me? What kind of game are you playing?'

'If you'd shut up for a minute instead of going off half-cocked, I'd tell you!' Royce shouted furiously, glaring back at her, rolling effortlessly to his feet. He slipped his hands into his pockets and threw his head back with an unconscious arrogance. 'I realise this is something of a shock to you. I meant to lead up to it, ply you with roses and champagne and candlelight dinners before I proposed. But seeing you with that baby in there hurried things up.' Her eyes smouldered. 'But you're too smart for all that, aren't you? It wouldn't have softened you up at all.'

'Oh, too right, Mr Drummond.' Her voice was clipped.

'So I simply took the bull by the horns and hoped to catch you off guard. I need a wife and, after tonight, I see you could certainly use a husband.'

'I don't believe I'm hearing this!' she gasped. 'Why would I need a husband?'

'To help you with your son, of course.'

'I've managed perfectly well without one up to now.' She walked stiffly to the door and held it open. 'Please leave, Mr Drummond. I'll pretend we never had this conversation.'

'I'm not leaving,' he said precisely, stepping close to her and slamming the door so hard the walls shook. 'I haven't said all I came to say.'

'I don't want to hear it!'

'You're going to listen.' He gripped her shoulders and shook her.

The terrycloth robe she wore was tied at the waist, but the violent way he shook her made it loosen and all at once it slipped open, parting the two sides. She tried to grab the edges and pull it together, but Royce blocked her efforts easily, and she stood paralysed with embarrassment as his eyes flared with something she couldn't name. They dropped to the front of her to enjoy the sight of her slender naked body, and she wanted to die with shame. A nerve twitched in his clenched jaw as one of his hands slipped inside the robe to rest on the warm curve of her hip.

Her heart stopped beating for a breathless moment before it began racing again in sudden panic. She was drawn closer until she felt the roughness of his clothes brushing against her, the warmth of his body reaching out to the burning heat of hers.

His other hand moved to her neck where it rested on her pounding pulse. Then his lips were there, feather-soft, lightly teasing, brushing her sensitive skin, and she thought she would faint from the sudden spinning sensations coursing through her.

She should have pulled away, but her body had a will of its own and wouldn't listen to her more practical mind.

This shouldn't be happening, it said. How could you let it? You'll be sorry.

But why not enjoy it for the moment? it answered. This is something that has never happened before and will never happen again.

Her eyes closed and a crazy weakness attacked her legs. She had the strangest sensation of floating yet being held fast and safe. Her head spun in dizzy spirals. She had never been so aware of any man before, aware of the hard strength of his arms, the silky softness of his coal black hair clinging to her fingers, the shape of his head, the warmth of his skin stretching across firm cheekbones and jutting jaw. An elusive masculine scent clung to his slightly damp skin and she felt herself drawn closer and closer until she must melt right into his body and become part of him.

Was this what Meg felt? she wondered. Finally she could understand the powerful attraction that had resulted in that beautiful baby in the other room. She had always wondered. Now she knew.

Giving herself a mental shake, she focused her dazed eyes on Royce and felt a furious heat coursing through her body all the way from her toes to the roots of her hair, now hanging wildly about her face.

She was on the sofa, draped all over him, but she had no idea how she got there. Her whole body clenched as she pulled herself together, dragging herself off him, standing on trembling legs, belting her robe tightly around her.

For a long moment they looked at each other in a thick and seething silence.

'Well, Jennifer? Will you marry me?' His voice was cool as he sat up and ran his fingers through his hair, trying to restore it to some kind of order.

Had she done that to him? Her chest rose and fell in a harsh agitated movement. She was out of breath and still slightly dazed. This total abandonment of all her senses was new to her. There was a curious ringing sensation in her ears, and she wondered who she was and where she was and how she came to be here.

'There's a passionate woman under all that ice,' Royce said softly, getting to his feet, stepping closer to her. 'I wasn't wrong. I want you for my wife. Marriage to me wouldn't be so bad, would it?'

Jenna jerked back automatically. 'It's impossible.'

'I know you're not indifferent to me. So why?'

She shook her head blindly from side to side. 'I

just can't. It's—it's preposterous. You don't really expect me to fall all over myself and accept?' He couldn't think that!

A black scowl crossed his features and his fists clenched. 'I need a wife.'

'I'm sure Meg would jump at the chance. Or Alexandra. Or Margo——'

'I want you!' he shouted furiously. 'If I wanted one of them, I'd have asked them. You're the only one who has all the qualifications I'm looking for.'

She stared at him, her eyes huge round blue saucers in her white face. 'You make it sound as if I'd passed an interview for a job!'

'You did, in a way. I need a paragon to fill the role of wife. You're practical and level-headed. You don't panic in unpleasant situations. If I asked you to entertain out-of-town guests at a moment's notice I'm sure you could do it.' His mouth twisted. 'That's the sort of thing I'm talking about. I can count on you. When you're in charge, everything runs smoothly. Nothing ruffles you.'

Jenna gaped at him. Didn't he know he ruffled her just by being in the same room with her?

'I realise after one disaster with a man, you're probably wary about stepping into another, but you're exactly the kind of woman I need for a wife.'

She closed her eyes for a long moment, expecting him to have vanished when she opened them again. This couldn't be happening! It was so much worse than her most horrible nightmare. This was like no proposal she had ever imagined.

When she opened her eyes again, he was still

there watching her. Shivers raced down her spine at the unreadable look in his smouldering eyes. An unconsciously held breath bubbled past her lips as she sank down into a chair and brushed a hand across her face. 'I'm sorry, Mr Drummond, it's just not possible.'

'Give me one good reason why.' He sounded furious.

'I'm old-fashioned, remember? Marriage involves love. And sharing. A commitment for life with trust and—and growth.' Jenna groped for a way to put her feelings into words.

'Did you feel that way when you had that baby in there?' Royce jeered harshly. 'Where was all the loving and sharing and trust then?'

'Just leave him out of it!'

'No.' He came closer and squatted on the floor in front of her, looking straight into her eyes. 'I want you and I know he goes along with you. You need someone to help you take care of him. Or are you waiting for his father to be free so you can marry him?'

Jenna sucked in a harsh breath and searched his face as if it would tell her how much he knew.

'Meg told me the man was married and you never told him about the baby, but she wouldn't say any more than that.' He took her small cold hands in his. 'I don't care about any of that. It's in your past. I'm your future. If you marry me, I can give you security, a beautiful home to live in, a family to care for your son.'

Her shallow breathing stopped altogether. 'I couldn't sell myself for those things.'

His face hardened to granite, his jaw clenched and he lost a little of his colour as a sudden stillness fell between them. 'Then what will you sell yourself for? Name your price. Whatever it is, I'll meet it.'

Jenna tried to twist her hands away from him, but his fingers tightened, crushing them. 'I haven't got a price!' she cried. 'I'm not like the other women you date. When I give something, there's no strings attached. And when I'm given anything, I expect the same. I work for you, Mr Drummond, and you pay me a good wage for that work. That's all there is between us. That's all there can ever be. Take your violets and get out of here!'

'All right, then, I'll keep it strictly business.' His mouth twisted. 'Right now I'm paying you to be my secretary. I'll double your salary if you'll be my wife. And don't worry, you'll earn every penny you're paid.'

Totally at a loss, she stared at him. 'You'd *pay* me to be your wife? Why? I'm sure any one of a dozen women would jump at the chance.'

'But not you.'

A deep frown creased her forehead and her bright blue eyes were bewildered. 'I don't understand you at all. You've got all kinds of women throwing themselves at you all the time.'

'But not you,' he said again. 'You're different. You're the kind of woman a man looks for when he wants a wife. They're the kind men take for lovers.'

The colour in her face deepened to a hot painful crimson and something seemed to shrivel inside her. 'Oh, I see. You want someone to blend into the background, someone you can take for granted, to be there for your convenience when you need her and invisible when you don't.'

With his head bent, Royce stared at her hands crushed in his for a long moment, his face unreadable, then he gave her a long measuring look. 'I wouldn't have put it quite so baldly, but yes—I need that kind of wife. Any passion between us would have been a fringe benefit. But it's not necessary. I can get it elsewhere. I need someone to help me raise my brothers and sisters, and you're the only one I can ask.'

He let her hands go and she flexed her fingers one by one, glad to feel the tingling sensation as the blood rushed back through them. The pain was real. She wasn't imagining this idiotic conversation.

'Would you care to sit down and explain?' she finally said, willing herself to listen. It was ridiculously absurd, but she might as well hear him out. For a horrified moment earlier she thought he was playing some kind of cruel game, leading her on to see how soon he could make her capitulate before he told her it was all a joke. Handsome men didn't make passes at plain girls—let alone propose! But his face was serious enough and she doubted he was a good enough actor to fake those bluish lines at the corners of his mouth.

He got to his feet, then sank wearily down on the sofa, dragging his hands through his hair, facing her across the small span of the living room. 'You're aware that I'm the eldest of seven children?'

This was news to her, but she kept her face expressionless, nodding as if she had known it all along. After all, if she had ever really met Peter, he probably would have mentioned it.

'I'm thirty-three, Jennifer. Peter's next at twenty-five. Then there's Kathleen who's nineteen, Susan, seventeen, Ryan, fifteen, and the twins, Adam and Zachary, who are thirteen. My father died ten years ago and, since I was the eldest, everything fell on me. It had to. I've never regretted the responsibility, and now they're more like my own children rather than brothers and sisters.'

Jenna blinked but didn't say anything. He was presenting a different picture of himself, that of a responsible family man rather than irresponsible playboy. Had she misjudged him? She shook her head. No, there were all those roses . . .

'My mother's about to remarry,' he said quietly, '—a hotelier from the Bahamas. For days now, all I've had is chaos at home. They're impressionable teenagers and they don't want to move to an island with a stepfather. Visiting is all right, but they don't want to live there, and he can't sell up and move here because it's a family business and he's put his whole life into it.

'The twins have threatened to run away. Susan says she'll marry the first man who asks her. Ryan's been hounding all his friends for a spare room in their homes. Kathleen's in the middle of her university training and says it's unfair to ask her to transfer. Peter's the only one who's unaffected, because he and his wife are off somewhere in Mexico and don't know anything about it.'

Jenna felt herself sympathising with him, but had to check the impulse. It simply wouldn't do.

'My mother's a nervous wreck.' Royce grabbed his head as if it ached. 'She's thinking now of calling the wedding off because it's not right for her to be happy at the expense of her children.' His luminous eyes pleaded with her. 'The only workable solution I could come up with is to find a suitable wife and settle down to care for them, since I've been doing it all these years anyway. My mother keeps telling me it's high time I married, and I'm not getting any younger.'

'But that would put quite a crimp in your style, wouldn't it?' she said slightly.

A relieved look crossed his face. 'I knew you'd understand. I need someone to be there in the evenings, after work and on weekends when I'm not. Someone reliable, to take my mother's place.'

'Why don't you just hire a housekeeper? You don't need to tie yourself down with a wife.'

'We have a housekeeper, but she absolutely refuses to be responsible for five teenagers. She says it's enough to ask her to keep the house running smoothly without trying to have her keep track of five wild Indians too. But you could do it. Nothing bothers you. If you married me, I wouldn't be tied down. I'd still have my own life—discreetly, of course. I wouldn't humiliate you. We don't have to pretend to anyone that there's any love between us, but I think we could get on well together—like an old married couple. I'll provide for you and your son. You'll be paid well. And in return, you'll care for my family and home as efficiently as you do the office.'

Jenna reeled from his unthinking selfishness. Did he actually believe she'd go along with this absurd idea? That she'd let him have his cake and eat it too? Didn't he realise she had feelings and wants and needs, not to mention a son who was his nephew?

'Will you at least think about it?' He injected a touch of pleading in his voice when he saw her darkening frown.

'There's nothing to think about. I sympathise with you—but no. It's the most absurd proposal I've ever heard!'

'Oh? Have you heard many?' He arched one black mocking eyebrow upward.

Ice began moving over her again. He knew no one had ever asked her to marry him before, but she had pride. Some day a man just might fall in love with her. It wasn't all that impossible. All girls had that hope, even the plain ones, even the most liberated, even if they would never admit it. What kind of life was he offering her compared to what she hoped for?

'I'm sorry, the answer is still no.' Besides, there was the added complication of Meg—Meg, the sister she was responsible for, the sister who wanted Royce for herself. She could just imagine her reaction if she told her Royce had proposed.

'Don't be so quick to refuse.' He rolled to his feet in an easy motion and stood facing her, a coaxing smile on his handsome face. 'I know I've done this badly, but you're a practical person. Take some time to weigh the pros and cons. Think of what I'm offering you and your son: the Drummond name and a chance for respectability, if nothing else. You'll have to look long and hard for another man to accept an illegitimate son with no questions asked.'

Her heart twisted painfully. If he only knew. . .

'I don't have to think about it, Mr Drummond. The answer has to be no.'

'You'll think about it,' he said softly, reaching out to brush his fingertips swiftly down the side of her face in an unbearably sensuous caress that ended almost before it began. 'You're tempted, my paragon. It's there in your eyes. You won't be able to stop thinking about it.'

CHAPTER FIVE

HE was right. His absurd proposal took precedence over every other thought she had. All through her working day it buzzed like a persistent fly at the back of her brain. She couldn't seriously consider it, she told herself. It was the most ridiculous thing she'd ever heard. But she couldn't forget it.

Royce Drummond knew it too. He watched her, silently, knowingly, with the utmost patience. He didn't mention it again, made no sly references, no innuendoes, but Jenna knew he was waiting for her to come and tell him she was ready to accept. She simply had to. After all, as plain as she was, she'd never get a better offer. He must have thought he was irresistible—or rather, his name, position and wealth were. But he hadn't realised how much truth there was in his statement that she was different from the rest of the women he knew.

When, after a week, she still hadn't literally fallen into his arms, he changed his tactics.

At five o'clock one rainy evening at the beginning of June, Jenna straightened her papers on her desk and was putting the cover on her typewriter when a hesitant voice came floating across the wide room.

'Excuse me. Is Royce still here?'

She watched a tall young man advance. He was dressed in well-worn blue jeans and a dripping grey sweatshirt. He had obviously been caught unprepared for the rain, his white canvas shoes were muddy and squelched with each step, but he didn't stop until he was at her desk. His hair was soaking wet and standing on end and he brushed the droplets out of his eyes with an impatient hand, inadvertently showering her in the process.

There was no denying he was one of Royce Drummond's brothers. He had the same smoky grey eyes and finely chiselled features as her employer, but he was much thinner, almost gangly, and she didn't think he was through growing yet.

'Ryan?' she asked, taking a wild guess.

He grinned, nodding. 'And you have to be Jennifer. Royce told us all about you. You're everything he said—and more.' He bowed regally, but all at once he made a sudden awkward movement and jerked his hand over her desk to take one of hers, swiftly planting a wet kiss on the back of it.

He took her so much by surprise that after a stunned moment, she wanted to burst out laughing. Controlling herself with an effort, she turned crimson.

He must have thought she'd become enraged, because he straightened abruptly and took a quick step backward. 'Royce said to be charming.' He blinked and shifted uncomfortably, frowning. 'Didn't I do it right?'

The laugh she was trying to hold back gurgled in her throat before spreading across her face in a wide grin. 'You did it perfectly. You're just a couple hundred years too late, that's all. Men don't kiss girls' hands any more. And they certainly don't track mud across her carpet!'

'Royce'll kill me,' he muttered, dejectedly slumping his shoulders. 'I was supposed to make a good impression and let you see our family isn't so bad. How about if I go out and come back in and try again?'

'I'll give you some advice, Ryan,' she said gently, trying her best not to laugh, 'in case the occasion to be charming ever comes up again. Wipe your feet if they're muddy—and as for the rest, if you just be yourself and do what comes naturally, you won't have any trouble. You were very gallant just now, but it wasn't an honest gesture.' She raised her voice a little so the man sure to be listening on the other side of the door would hear. 'Most girls appreciate honesty. They can spot a phoney a hundred yards away, and nothing turns them off faster. You'll find Royce in there.' She pointed to his office and reached for her raincoat and umbrella before leaving him, chuckling softly.

The next morning no mention of the incident was made, but the carpet had been cleaned and she wondered how Ryan had weathered his brother's wrath. She hoped he hadn't got into too much trouble. He seemed like a nice boy. He had a likeable open manner and a very appealing smile. There was something endearing about the way he thought to be charming.

Royce was in a good mood, although he kept her unusually busy all day. Once or twice he commented on how well they worked together in spite of their differences. In just these few short months she had come to anticipate his every thought and need. Reports from the file cabinets were ready and waiting on his desk almost before he asked for them and he let her know he appreciated it.

When she waited for him to start his dictation that afternoon, she felt his eyes on her and when she looked up from her pad with her pencil poised, she caught a look of quiet speculation in his eyes as if he wondered if she could read his mind. Warm colour touched her face but she didn't say anything. She knew they'd never have this same rapport outside the office.

Later that afternoon the low grey clouds disappeared and the sun began to shine when Royce was called to another department to look over a new ad layout.

Using this time, she left her office and went to the stockroom to replenish her dwindling supplies. Her arms were piled high with typing paper, letterheads, ribbons, carbon and folders when she came back and fumbled with the firmly closed door to her office. She was sure she had left it open. Just as she had opened it again, two boys appeared from nowhere, startling her.

'Here, let me help you.'

'That looks heavy. Let me take these . . .'

Before she could protest, each grabbed for the papers she was balancing. One began to push at the things on top while the other pulled from the bottom. Jenna, caught in the middle, lost her grip on all of it and all at once everything went flying.

She looked at the mess scattered on the floor, then at the two who caused it. Consternation crossed her face and she started to say something, but thought better of it, clamping her mouth tightly shut in a hard thin line.

They were twins, identical, with very dark

brown hair and big blue eyes and the same
sheepish expressions on their handsome faces.
They weren't dressed alike. One wore navy blue
cords and the other jeans, but they both had
bright blue sweat shirts with the sleeves pushed
back to the elbows.

'Don't tell me,' she said at last. 'Adam and
Zachary.'

A small smile spread across one face. 'I'm
Zachary.' The smile turned to a bright white
grin. 'This is my brother Adam. We're pleased to
meet you, Jennifer. You're everything Royce said
you were.'

Adam, being closer to her, grabbed her hand
and started pumping up and down. 'We're
sorry about the mess, but we'll help you pick it
up.'

'You're not trying to get water out of her!'
Zachary's tone was full of exasperation as he
elbowed his brother out of the way and smiled an
apology. 'You'll have to forgive him. He's not so
good at being charming.'

'At least I didn't try to kiss her hand,' Adam
flashed with a scathing toss of his head.

Jenna's irritation fled as a tiny laugh stopped
somewhere in the middle of her throat, coming
out as a strangled cough instead. 'It's a pleasure
to meet you both, I think. Why don't you have a
seat in my office until your brother comes back?
He's at a meeting right now.' Her expression
narrowed a little. 'Or did you come to see me?'

The boys guiltily looked at each other and just
as guiltily looked away.

'Er—we were downtown doing some shopping
and thought we'd see if Royce could take us

home. How about if we just get to know each other until he comes back?'

She glanced at their empty hands. 'It doesn't look as if your shopping trip was very successful.'

'They didn't have the right size.'

'They didn't have the right colour.'

Both boys spoke at once and looked pained when their excuses differed.

But Zachary was the quickest to cover up the blunder. 'We were looking for jackets. They had my size but the wrong colour. Adam found the right colour but the wrong size.'

Jenna tilted her head to the side and looked them up and down, trying to keep her expression bland but a knowing smile danced in her eyes. 'It's too bad you couldn't have traded with each other. I thought twins were pretty much the same size.

Adam opened his mouth to try to come up with another explanation, but Zachary immediately sent him a glowering look that told him they weren't dealing with an imbecile.

'You've got us there,' he said softly, admitting defeat.

Jenna got down on her hands and knees and began picking up the papers, trying to hide a wide grin. They might not think Ryan was very good at being charming, but subtlety wasn't their strong suit either. 'Put these on the desk for me, will you, Adam?' She handed him several bulky folders. 'And you, Zachary, how about picking up these ribbons?'

When everything was piled on to her desk in a messy heap, she motioned for them to sit down and settled herself in her chair. Her curiosity was aroused and a smile lurked at the corners of her mouth, but she stayed silent, letting them make the first move.

Shrinking in their chairs, they hung their heads as if expecting a reprimand. When none came, Zachary dared to look up through his dark lashes, but there was nothing contrite in his eyes. They were too full of mischief. Then he folded his arms across his chest and relaxed in his chair, and she knew she was in for it.

'So, how do you like working for my brother?' he asked with an attempt at nonchalance that made her smile turn to a grin.

'He's a challenge,' she said softly.

'He treats you well?'

'As well as most employers treat their secretaries.'

'He pays you a good wage?'

She nodded. 'Very generous.'

He took his time digesting this. 'Then you probably wouldn't be as happy with anyone else, would you?'

'Is there some question of my leaving?' Her eyebrows rose.

'Oh no,' Adam interrupted quickly. 'He doesn't mean that at all. Royce said you'd still work here after you married him. He told us he couldn't run this office without you. Besides, he knows you're a liberated woman with a baby of your own, so he wouldn't ask you to stay at home and have his babies, the way most ... ordinary ...' he faltered and his voice trailed away uncertainly when he saw a bright red flush run into her face.

'Now you've gone and done it!' Zachary

snapped irritably, throwing an exasperated look at his brother. 'I told you to let me do the talking.' He turned back to Jenna, straightening for the attack, but before a word come out of his open mouth. Adam cut in.

'I was only trying to soften her up and let her know she wasn't going to have to give up this job. Susan intends to babysit for her son. Royce said he didn't know if he made that clear when he proposed.'

Zachary visibly winced and gritted his teeth, looking as if he'd like to pound his brother. Ignoring Jenna altogether, he began to shout. 'You dummy! You're supposed to use finesse. You don't go blundering in, talking about her son and telling her how liberated she is. You've got to be subtle and beat around the bush for a while. Make it sound like a compliment instead of an accusation. What's the matter with you? Hasn't watching Royce trying to make it with girls all these years taught you anything?'

Adam coloured painfully and nudged Zachary sharply in the ribs, motioning in Jenna's direction with a toss of his head, trying to remind him she was there listening to every word they said. 'You're dumb yourself,' he muttered under his breath. 'You're not supposed to let her know how many girls he's had.'

They both stopped arguing and looked at her.

Finally Zachary said contritely, 'Sorry, I guess we blew it too. Maybe worse than Ryan did yesterday.'

'Not at all, boys.' Jenna let out a small sigh. 'I couldn't work for your brother and not know what a ladies' man he is.' Her fingers sifted through a small stack of papers on her desk. 'These are florists' receipts for this month's roses he's had me send to his different women.'

'Wow!' Zachary's eyes rounded with surprise.

'No wonder you don't want to marry him,' Adam said shrewdly. 'Exactly how many women does he have, anyway?'

She shrugged. 'I don't waste my time counting them. They change from week to week anyway. I just send them roses, note their preferences when it comes to jewellery and jot down their messages when they ring here. It all goes in one ear and out the other.'

Adam grimaced slightly and she could see a flare of compassion come and go in his eyes. 'He calls you his paragon. Now I see why. I don't think any other secretary would put up with that.'

'Oh, you'd be surprised,' she said softly. 'There are a lot of men like him.'

He looked at her for a long moment, weighing what she said. He shook his head and pounded a fist against the arm of his chair and when he finally spoke his voice was ragged. 'How could he be so selfish? He was wrong to insult you with a proposal of marriage. You're too good for him!' He jumped to his feet and stood breathing heavily. 'Come on, Zack. I'm not waiting around for Royce.'

With a slightly confused frown, Zachary looked from him to Jenna and then back again. 'I think I missed something.'

'I'll explain it on the way home,' he said shortly. 'Goodbye, Jennifer. I'm glad we had this chance to meet you.'

She gave him a troubled nod, watching them leave, biting her lip. Somehow she didn't think that had turned out quite the way any of them expected. But how was she to know Adam would be so sensitive?

As she began to clear her desk, a sudden trickle of apprehension slithered down her spine. Lifting her chin, she looked straight into condemning, icy grey eyes.

'Thanks, Paragon!' Royce ground out savagely before he slammed the door between their offices so hard it rattled the windows.

From the murderous look on his face she knew he had been in his office the whole time and had heard everything. Feeling somehow to blame even though she knew she wasn't, she numbly finished clearing her desk and then typed out a short terse page, not giving herself time to think about what she was doing. It had been building a long time. Now her actions became automatic, all sensation flat and dead.

With a soft knock on the office door, she pushed it open and silently crossed the room to stand before her employer's desk.

Royce was sitting stiffly in his high-backed swivel chair, absorbed in the papers in his hands, a brooding scowl on his handsome face when she smoothly settled the resignation she had typed on top of the other papers he was holding.

He did not look up, and his scowl deepened as he read it in silence.

It stretched endlessly between them, but Jenna rigidly stood her ground without speaking, waiting.

Finally he found his voice. 'Why?'

'I won't come between you and your family, Mr Drummond. This will be best for all of us.'

'I won't accept it.' Standing, he ripped it in two, never taking his burning eyes off her. 'You heard my brothers. I can't run this office without you.'

'That's not true and you know it. It was an empty compliment meant to flatter me.'

'Isn't that just great?' he exploded. 'Am I supposed to applaud you because you've got your head sitting square on your shoulders? Come down off of your high and mighty perch long enough to see what's happened here! Adam's been hurt. And you're the one who hurt him. You're not walking away now and leaving me to pick up the pieces all by myself. You'll stay and you'll help me!' It wasn't a request; it was a command.

Her mouth fell open as she stared at him, anger flashing in her eyes. '*I* didn't hurt him, Royce Drummond. *You* did. You, with your string of conquests—and your bloody roses!'

'For God's sake!' He came right around his desk and stood close to her, his own anger vibrating all around them. 'Why do you have to make such a production out of everything? Why can't you be like every other woman I've ever known?'

'Never!' she shouted. 'They don't have the sense to see how you despise them. I won't be used and then discarded like all the rest!'

'But I've asked you to marry me—I thought I made that clear. You won't be discarded. It wouldn't be just a brief affair.'

'No, you'd rather give me a sham of a

marriage.' She was numb with outrage, her eyes blazing in her white face. 'It's the rest of my life we're talking about, not some weekend fling. The answer was no before. It's still no.'

'I'll triple your salary.'

Stunned, she stood absolutely still, staring straight into grey eyes glazed with a strange sheen of ice. 'How dare you!' she choked.

A muscle was working furiously in his jaw and he looked ready to explode. 'Can't you see? I'm not the only one who'll benefit from this marriage. As my wife, you'll have a claim to everything I own. You know I'm a wealthy man.'

'I wouldn't marry you for all the money in the world.' Her voice was deadly calm.

All his taut muscles began to relax and his shoulders slumped. 'If you won't think of me, think of my mother. She's desperate. You have to help me help her—you're the only one who can.' His hands came up to grip her shoulders, unthinkingly crushing her slender bones. 'How can I reach you? I've offered you everything I own, but you keep turning me down. I thought my family could plead their case better than I could. After all, I'm doing this for them, not for myself. They're only children, but they know you're their only hope. They offered to come and talk to you.' He bit back a sharp sigh. 'All I've done is complicate things, haven't I? *God*!' The cry came from deep in his throat and was husky and full of despair.

He stood for a long taut moment staring with a desperate kind of pleading, his eyes glowing like polished bits of steel, roaming over her face with a hungry brilliance. His hands clenched on her shoulders and she could see he was struggling with himself. 'Jennifer,' he muttered in a shaken voice. 'Jennifer!'

Jenna watched in fascination as his face came down to hers. Mesmerised, she didn't think to turn away. His hands gentled on her shoulders, curving right around her, gathering her close, enfolding her in a warm encompassing embrace before his lips parted hers.

All resistance fled, giving way to desires she had never known before, and she was swept away on a swiftly rising tide of terrifying sweetness. She wouldn't have been surprised had he been rough or ruthless or demanding, but this tenderness was her complete undoing.

A strange curling sensation began in the pit of her stomach, radiating to the rest of her before dissolving her bones in a treacherous flooding weakness. Without realising it, she clung to him, her hands hesitating only for an instant before stealing up around his neck and sliding through the thick black silk of his hair. The blood sang in her ears when she felt his whole body quivering as he moulded her slender length against his, his hands warm and firmly caressing on the small of her back, holding her firmly to him.

The merest thread of a sound, almost a gasp, reached her consciousness before Royce stiffened, lifting his face away from hers, tilting his head to a listening angle. The door between the two offices stood open, but it was empty.

Then all at once someone in the outer office was noisily clearing his throat and jingling the coins in his pocket to let them know they were not alone.

Jenna broke away from him guiltily and smoothed her hands down the sides of her skirt, hoping she didn't look as heated as she felt. He dragged his hands through his hair, looking strangely embarrassed, and for a moment their eyes met, hers full of unanswerable questions, his naked and unguarded, revealing enough to tell her everything she wanted to know if only she'd been experienced enough to read them.

They were still, breathless, staring at one another, then Chad Redwicke appeared in the doorway followed by a tall, slender, white-haired woman, and the fleeting moment passed as they both turned towards them.

'Royce, I met this charming woman in the hallway asking for directions to your office.' He smiled then and arched an eyebrow in Jenna's direction.

She shuddered, knowing he had seen them and knowing it was only a matter of time before everyone else in the building heard about it.

'Thanks for showing her in.' Royce cleared his throat, banishing its husky tremor.

'Hello, dear. Won't you introduce me before this charming young man has to go back to his work?' The woman smiled serenely, her grey gaze narrowing on Royce's look of discomfiture and the hectic colour running into Jenna's face. She chattered on before he had a chance to do as she asked. 'The children finally told me what you've been up to and I just had to come and see for myself what my prospective daughter-in-law looks like.'

Jenna's heart fell down to her shoes. That was all Chad had to hear! Five minutes after he left this office, the whole building would be buzzing. She looked murderously at Royce, willing him to explain that she wasn't going to marry him, but he quickly seized the opportunity and smiled.

'Mother, I'd like you to meet Jennifer Caldwell, my secretary, soon to be my wife.'

'How lovely to meet the woman who's finally tamed my son,' she smiled, offering her hand to Jenna.

'How do you do, Mrs Drummond,' Jenna said shakily, putting her hand in hers. 'But Royce is wrong. I'm not——'

He cut her off quickly with the other introduction. 'And this is Chad Redwicke, Mother, one of our best illustrators.'

'The pleasure's all mine, ma'am,' Chad beamed at her, shaking her hand and nodding with a practised flourish before turning to Jenna. 'May I be one of the first to offer congratulations? I should have known you'd set your sights higher than the graphic department. What do they always say? It's the quiet ones you have to watch, or something like that.'

She cringed at his acid tone and saw the sudden rigid stiffening of Royce's body out of the corner of her eye, but she couldn't keep silent. 'There are no congratulations in order, Chad. I turned him down, and I also handed in my resignation.'

'*What?*' Both he and Mrs Drummond spoke at once.

Her eyes flashed with triumph. 'You explain it, Royce,' she said sweetly, turning on her heel to leave them.

But he reached out and clamped a hand on her

wrist, dragging her back to him, smiling a hateful silky smile that didn't reach his eyes. 'A mere lovers' quarrel, but nothing I can't handle,' he drawled, crushing her wrist when she tried to struggle away, pulling her back against his long heated length.

Her whole body burned where his touched hers and she wanted to scream with frustration, but she knew she was beginning to look ridiculous.

Royce nodded a dismissal to Chad and smiled at his mother. 'Won't you sit down? I'm sure Jennifer's dying to tell you all the reasons why she doesn't want to marry me.'

CHAPTER SIX

Mrs Drummond took an appraising look at both of them, then seated herself on the comfortable sofa, setting her handbag on the low table in front of her. For such a tall woman, she looked particularly fragile in a rose linen dress, but she lifted her head and there was a look of determination on her pleasant face. As she patted the cushion beside her, her bright grey eyes sparkled with something Jenna couldn't name. 'Come and talk to me,' she said quietly. 'I assure you I don't bite.'

Royce released Jenna's wrist and gave her a small push towards his mother. She nervously unclenched her hands and brushed back several wisps of hair falling across her eyes, gratefully sinking down on to the sofa, trying to pull herself together. Her hands were still shaking when she noticed her blouse had come loose from the waistband of her dark skirt and she hurriedly tried to tuck it in.

'What have you been doing to this poor child, Royce?' his mother accused gently. 'Caveman tactics may be all right for some, but this fragile flower needs delicate treatment.'

'She only looks fragile. She's a lot more resilient than any of us think.'

Mrs Drummond's eyebrows rose as she looked from one to the other and then she noticed the light of resentment in Jenna's eyes. 'You shouldn't have let my son in on one of our best kept secrets,' she chuckled. 'He'd much rather think of a woman as a simpering idiot whose one aim in life is to find a man to take care of her than one who's able to take care of herself.'

'She values her independence too much to ever let herself lean on a man,' Royce cut in.

'What's wrong with that?' Jenna grated.

'Everything's wrong with it. You've got your son to think of. He suffers from choking bouts of bronchitis, but will you see that my offer will help him too? No,' he answered his own question with a sneer, 'you're too stubborn to admit this marriage would be good for both of you. You've refused me point blank—probably hoping I'll think you're wonderful for standing on your own two feet.'

'You beast!' she snapped furiously, glaring at him. 'You're turning it all around on purpose to humiliate me in front of your mother! You know there's more to it than that.' Her fists curled, the nails digging deeply into her palms, her breathing quickening as she sprang to her feet.

But Royce was right there waiting for her, looking down at her with blazing eyes, his breathing, like hers, swift and shallow. It seemed an age before he moved, coming closer to her, their bodies almost touching.

Jenna wanted to step back, but her legs refused to move. Her heart hammered noisily in her ears and their eyes locked together. Every clamouring nerve in her body reached out to him. Why can't I think straight when he's near me? she thought wildly. Why can't I resist him? Her body betrayed her and, unnerved by his nearness, she began to quiver uncontrollably, swaying towards him.

She forgot his mother sitting there watching them. She forgot her surroundings. She was only conscious of him and her senses started to swim. The heated scent of his body enveloped her and in spite of herself she wanted again to feel his body against hers, touch the warm rippling muscles in his chest, stroke his thick silky hair and watch it cling to her fingers, taste his mouth on hers. A sudden warmth swept through her, an increasing urgency beginning in her stomach and uncurling to every nerve end.

Watching her, his eyes changed, narrowing to diamond-bright pinpoints, and then she realised he could see everything. She was telling him things she wouldn't even admit to herself. To love him was sheer insanity! He would take her heart and soul and give only his meaningless wealth in return. In the end it would be an unfair exchange. Oh no, she thought, not me. Never me.

Swallowing back a bitter sob, she searched for her pride, trusting her chin up higher than necessary. 'Oh, I hate you!'

Royce laughed softly at first, not drawing away from her. But then, at the swift rush of blood coming into her face, he threw his head back and laughed mockingly. 'Oh no, my passionate paragon. You want to, but you don't hate me.'

'Go to h——' She remembered his mother sitting there and bit the word off just in time.

'Now, now,' he grinned, 'you mustn't let your mother-in-law see what a temper you've got!'

She glared at him in reckless fury, but he stepped away and nodded at his mother.

'Since you're obviously here to see Jennifer, I'll leave you two ladies to get acquainted. If you need me, I'll be in Accounting.'

Jenna threw daggers into his back long after he was gone.

After a moment Mrs Drummond cleared her throat and softly chuckled. 'I never would have credited my son with such exceptional taste, my dear. I always thought he'd choose someone more . . .' she hesitated, '. . . more worldly.'

'You mean glamorous,' she said without rancour. 'Don't forget, I've seen the women he dates.'

Her eyes twinkled. 'Royce has no secrets from you, has he?'

Jenna shook her head and sank down on the sofa with a slow defeated sigh. No, she thought, I know how depraved he is.

'Cheer up, my dear. It's much better to start off a marriage with your eyes wide open. That way there'll be no unpleasant shocks waiting for you.'

'I can't marry him, Mrs Drummond,' Jenna insisted.

'Nonsense.' She settled herself more comfortably and folded her hands in her lap. 'It's quite obvious you love him.'

Stiffening, Jenna jerked around to stare hard at her with wounded eyes. 'Is it obvious?' She was shocked. Only a moment ago she had come face to face with it and hated herself for it. But it was still too new—and too absurd.

'Only to me, my dear. But then I'm partial to my son.' Mrs Drummond patted her hand gently.

'I can't marry him,' she said desperately, her

face whitening. 'It's impossible. Believe me, there are—reasons.'

'I've heard that love covers a multitude of sins.'

'Love!' she choked. 'When two people marry, it's the love they have for each other that holds them together. Your son and I haven't got that. If anything, he feels sorry for me because he thinks I can't get a man of my own. He doesn't love me.'

'Perhaps not yet,' the older woman said quietly. 'But he cares about you and trusts you. That's a start. Maybe in time it will become love.'

'He's got an overdeveloped sense of responsibility, that's all. I'd only be a burden to him—and an embarrassment.'

Soft grey eyebrows rose in astonishment. 'Why? Because you have a son?'

Jenna dropped her face in her hands and her shoulders sagged. The more she talked, the deeper she got. 'It's not only that. Just look at me, Mrs Drummond.' She lifted her ravaged face to the woman. 'I'm not his type at all.'

'You could be a beautiful girl with the right clothes and cosmetics and haircut,' she said gently. 'And being an unmarried mother is nothing to punish yourself for.'

'You don't understand. I'm not——' Breathing in sharply, fighting back the words, Jenna shuddered. How could she even begin to explain her innocent involvement in all this? If she told her about Meg, she might try to force Royce to marry Meg instead. They'd take Robbie, and where would that leave her? For ever on the outside looking in? 'I just can't marry him,' she said again.

'If Royce didn't think you were right for him, I'm sure he wouldn't have asked you. He must feel comfortable with you. Once he told me that's why he never married—he never could find a woman he was comfortable with.'

'Please——'

'I don't want to be an interfering mother-in-law, but can't you see he needs you? I was so afraid he'd pick some floozy for a wife. You're so much more than I'd ever hoped for. I can't believe his good taste. You're just the one to make him put his philandering ways behind him.'

'Oh, Mrs Drummond, I'm the last person in the world to try to exert that kind of influence over him. I'm no good for your family. I've caused trouble between him and Adam already. It would only get worse if I even considered marriage.' There was another brother, Peter, involved, but Janna couldn't tell her that.

Mrs Drummond smiled knowingly. 'I think you're trying to paint yourself as quite a scarlet woman, but anyone looking at you could tell you're not promiscuous. A mistake can happen to anyone. Anyway, people are pretty broadminded in this day and age.'

'I can't marry him—take my word for it. It's just too much to ask!'

She searched Jenna's stricken face with narrowed eyes that must have seen something else. Then she slowly let out her breath and said very quietly, 'Because Royce insulted you with an offer of money?'

Jenna's face burned. 'He expected me to agree to it. *Expected* it! What kind of woman would accept money in return for marriage?'

'That's exactly what I told him. But you must remember, my dear, he's a businessman first, and the women he's dated up to now have been mercenary. He thought it was the only way to reach you. But you've got integrity and you'll make him see how wrong he is.'

'He won't see it. I suit his convenience, that's all.'

'I know you've been offended, but if you can overlook it and simply marry him because you love him, he'll see that there really is a good woman in this world. He'll come to love you. You'll be his salvation.'

For a long time Jenna just sat there. If only there was some way to get through to Mrs Drummond without hurting her!

'What else is bothering you, Jennifer? It's not just the matter of his convenience or his offer of payment. You're a practical girl—he told me that much. You're not some blind romantic. Won't you tell me?'

'It would only hurt you.'

'I haven't lived all these years without knowing hurt. Tell me what's really stopping you from marrying my son. I'm sure you love him enough to overlook any insult he might have made. What is it? I want you to trust me with the truth. If you're completely honest, whatever it is, I can accept it.'

Jenna looked at her with tortured eyes. She couldn't come right out with it.

'Please my dear.'

She shuddered defeatedly. 'It was my sister Meg who had the baby, not me. I've never known——' her face burned, '—anyway, I'd made a promise to my mother to take care of Meg and when I found out she was pregnant, I felt it was my fault. I'd failed them both. Meg didn't want a baby, but I wouldn't hear of an abortion. I thought once she saw him . . . held him . . .' Salty tears stung her eyes. 'But it didn't work out that way. I'm the one who loves him . . .'

Mrs Drummond blinked, slightly dazed, searching her face for long seconds. 'How very magnanimous of you, my dear, but why should that cause you such a problem? If you told Royce what you've told me, I'm sure he'd understand. Why, it might even make things easier between you.'

'No, it wouldn't.'

Mrs Drummond kept looking at her, frowning, trying to read her closed expression. 'There's something else, isn't there?'

Jenna's clenched hand was pressed against her mouth and her face was a ghastly white.

'I want to know, my dear,' she prodded.

Those ruthlessly probing eyes never left her face and finally, with a short sigh of inevitability, Jenna got to her feet and went to her office to bring back her wallet, flipping through it until she came to a recent picture of Robbie. Handing it to Mrs Drummond, she waited.

Tilting her head to a questioning angle, the other woman took the picture from her with a small frown, then her eyes widened in a shock of puzzled recognition and her mouth fell open. For a few agonising seconds there was complete silence, then her tortured eyes sought Jenna's. 'He's Royce's son?' she whispered, blanching.

Jenna shook her head from side to side.

'Then—Peter's?' The name was torn from her throat. *'Peter's!'*

After a long moment her breath was harshly drawn in and she slowly got to her feet and walked to the wide windows behind her son's desk, staring blindly at the broad panorama of downtown Toronto, her back rigid, her head high. 'I have a grandson,' she said with a ragged catch in her stunned voice, 'and no one told me.'

'No one else knows.'

'Peter doesn't know he has a son?' She turned and looked at Jenna in a bewildered daze.

'Meg never told him she was pregnant. She knew he was married when—when they——And then he went off to Mexico, so he never knew. When Royce saw Robbie, he didn't recognise him.' Jenna drew in her breath in a trembling gulp. 'And I couldn't tell him.'

'Robbie.' The woman seemed to dwindle as she looked down at the picture she was still holding. 'Was he named after Peter's father?'

Pain splintered through Jenna when she saw the bright grey eyes fill with tears. 'I wish I could say yes, but no matter how many times I begged Meg to choose a name for him, she refused. I finally chose Robert, for no particular reason.'

Mrs Drummond smiled sadly, accepting it, and blinked back her tears, refusing to let them fall, drawing herself up to her full height, coming back to face Jenna squarely. 'He would have been proud to know his first grandson carried his name, even if it was unintentional.' Her face softened for just an instant and then she reached for her handbag. 'May I keep this picture?'

'Of course.'

'Thank you,' she whispered, turning swiftly to the door.

'Wait!' Jenna hesitated. 'What are you going to do?'

Mrs Drummond stopped but didn't turn around. 'Do?' she said quietly. 'Why, nothing. It's up to you, Jennifer.'

'You won't tell Royce?'

'No, I won't tell him. But you'll have to—preferably before you marry him.'

'But I can't marry him! Don't you see how impossible it is?'

'Peter's already married. The others are too young. That leaves only Royce.'

'But it wouldn't be fair to him,' Jenna said, aghast.

'You should have thought of that before you started pretending to be a mother.'

Ice shuddered down Jenna's spine and she made a helpless gesture. 'Mrs Drummond! I only told you all this because you asked me to be honest. Can't you see why it's impossible for me to marry him? If Royce—if he—if—he'd know in a minute I'd never had a baby. I thought you'd understand!'

'I understand I have a grandson who has a right to the Drummond name. Royce has offered it to him.'

'But I can't let him do that!'

'Shall I tell him he should marry your sister instead?' An incredulous silence fell between them before Mrs Drummond slowly turned, her face set in cold uncompromising lines. 'Or is she waiting for Peter's marriage to end? If she is, I'm afraid she'll be disappointed. I had a letter from him only last week saying he and Melanie have decided to try again to make to go of it. There's no other alternative. If you call yourself Robbie's mother, you'll have to marry Royce. I won't allow anything like this to interfere in Peter's life now that he's trying to put it back together. I'm sure Royce would agree with me.' Pain and disgust flickered over her face before she turned on her heel and abruptly walked away.

For almost five minutes after she left, Jenna stood where she was, unable to move or think or feel. And then reaction set in. Everything began to crowd in on her and her whole body began to tremble. She would have fallen if Royce hadn't walked in just then and caught her in his strong arms.

'What's happened?' he demanded.

She struggled as all sorts of conflicting emotions chased through her mind. 'Nothing,' she whispered, twisting out of his grasp. She couldn't think this close to him. She had to get away.

'Don't tell me that. I saw my mother in the hall. She hasn't looked that bad since the day my father died. What went on in here? Good God, I was only gone twenty minutes!'

Jenna was spared the necessity of answering by the strident ringing of the telephone. Seeing she was in no condition to answer it, Royce set her away from him, turning to his desk, and she made her escape.

CHAPTER SEVEN

JENNA knew it was only temporary. Sooner or later Royce had to find out about their nephew. She should have told him a long time ago. All she had done was make it that much more difficult.

After she had bathed Robbie and put him to bed, she sat in her tiny living room and went over her options. She could tell him the truth. Meg never really wanted Robbie, she heard herself telling him. I only told you he was mine because I love him and I was afraid you'd take him away from me. Besides, I was too proud and I didn't want you to think I was so plain I couldn't have a child of my own. She rejected that explanation at once—it exposed too much.

She could take Robbie and disappear. That action had merit. But once she thought it through, she saw it was cowardly. She had never run from anything before, and she wouldn't start now. The only way to solve a problem was to meet it head-on.

She could go ahead and marry Royce and not say anything. Theirs wouldn't be a real marriage anyway. He'd never know. But that was dishonest, and so unfair to him.

That led her back to her first option. She had to tell him the truth. But what if he took Robbie away from her and married Meg instead? How would she be able to stand it?

Her head spun and it was several seconds

before she realised the ringing in her ears was the doorbell.

A boy about fifteen years old stood there with a small white envelope in his hand. 'Jenna Caldwell?' he asked with a friendly smile. 'Your sister asked me to give you this.'

She closed the door for a second to release the chain lock before opening it again. 'Thank you,' she murmured with a slight frown, turning the envelope over and over in her hands.

'That's okay. She gave me ten dollars to make sure you got it tonight,' he said over his shoulder, turning to leave.

Jenna stared at his retreating back, then gasped slightly when she saw him stand aside to let two people pass him on the stairway. Mrs Drummond was on her way up, followed by Royce.

Her first impulse was to slam the door, but she realised how childish that would be. A feeling of inevitability washed over her as she stepped aside to let them into her flat without a word.

Royce nodded and looked quickly around before crossing to Robbie's bedroom. He silently pushed the door open as if looking for something, then came back to where his mother and Jenna was standing. 'You were wrong, Mother. He's sleeping and nothing's out of place. Now will you tell me why you thought she'd have disappeared tonight?'

Mrs Drummond sank down on a chair and fidgeted with her handbag, not looking at either of them. 'I'm glad I was wrong,' she whispered, staring blindly at the floor.

He ran a distracted hand through his hair. 'I'm sorry, Jennifer—I don't know what this is all about. My mother thought you and your baby would be gone when we got here.'

'Wishing she hadn't thought so badly of her, Jenna turned away, mangling the envelope in her hand.

He looked at it pointedly. 'Is that some kind of bad news? You're as white as a sheet.'

Blinking, she looked down at her twisting fingers. 'Oh,' she said softly, 'I don't know. It's from Meg. I haven't read it yet. Er—sit down, won't you? May I get you some coffee? Or tea?'

'No, thanks. Read your letter or whatever it is, then we'll clear up this great mystery between you and my mother.'

Jenna hesitated only a second, then tore it open. Meg's handwriting was bold and forceful and not a word was wasted.

Married Carlo Borchini this morning.
Honeymooning in Italy.

Meg

A slight gasp stopped in the middle of her throat, then all the breath went out of her. She just stood there not moving. Would her mother consider this her final failure?

Royce took the note from her unresisting fingers, frowning at her stricken face. 'May I?' He read it quickly, then tipped his head back, laughing silently at the ceiling. 'She told me she was going to marry money!' His soft chuckle became a laugh, then he slapped his hand against his thigh and let out a whoop. 'She knew she was wasting her time with me. I told her I was going to marry you, so she had to turn around and show me it didn't matter.

Well, good luck, Carlo, old boy. You're going to need it!'

'You told Meg?' Jenna gasped—and almost against her will she turned to look at Mrs Drummond.

The woman's head slowly lifted and a tense silence filled the space between them.

Royce couldn't read their faces and his smile faded. 'Yes, I told her. And she did exactly what I thought she'd do.' His lip curled. 'She's jealous of you, Jennifer. Did you know that? As beautiful as she is, she's jealous. And vindictive. She ranted and raved and even tried to tell me some story about your son not really being yours. Can you beat that?'

Her heart stopped and she dragged her eyes away from Mrs Drummond back to him. This is it, she thought, staring at his handsome face with the deep grooves slashing the sides of his mouth. I've lost him.

'Rubbish!' Mrs Drummond snapped, coming to stand close to her son. 'You didn't believe her?'

'I knew it was just her jealousy talking.'

'Well, good for you. I wouldn't have credited you with that much discernment.' At the surprised lift of his eyebrows, she went on, 'You're singularly obtuse when it comes to Jennifer. But never mind that. What else did Meg say about the child?'

'I wouldn't let her say anything else. Her raving turned into tears, and you know how much I like that. I left as fast as I could.'

Jenna watched Mrs Drummond's face crease into an almost triumphant smile and she felt a painful twisting in the middle of her chest, but she braced herself. It was all going to come out now. It had to.

She was trembling uncontrollably, but Mrs Drummond took her ice-cold hands in hers and looked deeply into her eyes, willing her to find the strength she needed. 'If you don't mind, I'll make some coffee while you explain things to Royce.' She crushed a piece of paper in her hands. 'Use this if you can't find the words.'

Jenna lowered her gaze and saw a document of some kind—and then her heart lurched when she realised it was Robbie's birth certificate. Turning the paper over and over in her hands, she felt cold and numb and close to tears. It was force of habit that made her blink back the stinging shimmer. She never cried. She wouldn't start now.

Royce was watching her curiously. He saw her pallor, her struggle to control the sudden bright moisture rushing to her eyes. 'Jennifer, is something wrong?'

Pulling herself together, she lifted her chin and faced him squarely as Mrs Drummond disappeared into the kitchen. 'I'm sorry if all this seems a little melodramatic, but I simply didn't know how to tell you. This afternoon I told your mother why I couldn't marry you, but she didn't want to accept my reasons.' It all came out in a rush, and then her voice faltered and she lost her nerve. Her throat closed up and she couldn't go on. Handing Royce the certificate, she let him read it for himself.

What struck her first was his stillness, then the greyness of his face and the trembling of his bunching fists.

'Oh, my God!' he choked in a dying whisper, before his hand came up as if he would strike her.

Without flinching, she stood there, waiting for the blow. It was all she deserved.

'Don't you dare hit a woman, Royce Drummond!' His mother's voice came from the doorway, firm and clear and decisive. 'I raised you better than that.'

'You knew! He's Peter's son and you didn't tell me!'

'It wasn't my place to tell you.'

A bitter hatred flashed across his face before he turned away, his features hardening into cold implacable granite. 'He always talked about Meg being so beautiful. I could have understood if he——' His eyes sought Jenna's, pinning her with a savage grey glitter. 'But you? What did he ever see in you?'

An involuntary gasp of pain escaped her before she dredged up a frozen poise. The look of fierce pride stealing over her face prompted Mrs Drummond to step in.

'That's quite enough, Royce. I have the coffee on a tray. Will you bring it in?'

Contempt flared in his eyes. 'Coffee? I think not.' Without another word, he turned on his heel and walked out of the door, slamming it hard behind him.

Something inside Jenna splintered. Her chin wobbled. She was close to crying, but she didn't want Mrs Drummond to see it. Forcing her head up, she squared her jaw and blinked furiously at the moisture in her eyes.

'I'm sorry, my dear,' Mrs Drummond said

gently. 'That's not quite what I expected from him.'

'If you'd let him hit me, it might have been better.'

'Nonsense. That would only add guilt to all the other emotions he's feeling right now.' She patted Jenna's shoulder and led her to a chair where she bent down and retrieved the birth certificate Royce had dropped. 'There was no way to break it to him gently. Once he comes to his senses he'll be all right.'

'It wasn't fair to hurt him like that.'

'You can still think of him after the way he insulted you?' Mrs Drummond marvelled. 'He doesn't know how lucky he is to have you love him.'

'Oh, please!'

'Your sister is a very selfish person, isn't she? Could you see my son married to a woman like her?'

Jenna shuddered and then remembered his taunt: *What did he ever see in you?* and her face flamed. 'I'm just as selfish, trying to keep Robbie for my own. If Meg hadn't run off with Carlo Borchini, she might have been able to get him to listen to her.'

Mrs Drummond watched her grimly. 'Your biggest trouble is a massive inferiority complex. You'll have to get over it, because we're in this together now.'

With a frown, Jenna looked at her standing so tall and still, holding out the paper to her. As she took it, one name leapt out at her as if it was written in blood. *Jennifer Caldwell.*

'But I don't understand!' she gasped.

'I didn't alter it, if that's what you're thinking. Your sister must have done it. What better way for her to shift her responsibility?' she said, her lips twisting. 'When I left you this afternoon I had to check on your story. It's a bit much to swallow. When I saw it, I thought you'd lied to me, but then I realised your sister must have been making sure she wouldn't be tied down with a baby she didn't want. I'll bet it killed her when she realised her selfishness had backfired.'

Jenna sat bolt upright, her eyes rounding. 'But this means——' She bit her lip and tried to check the sudden leaping of her heart. 'It would only be Meg's word against mine. Since my name is here—by law, *I'm* his mother! He's mine!'

'Actually, he's ours.' Mrs Drummond's voice was gentle but curiously cold. 'If you agree to marry Royce and give Robbie his rightful place in our family, I won't say a word. But if you don't, I'll tell Royce exactly what happened and have this document corrected.' She waited a moment to let the threat stand between them. 'He asked you to marry him to provide a stable environment for the rest of my family. Nothing's changed. Robbie's parentage has no bearing on that. If you won't agree, I'll have to fight you. And where will that leave you?'

Jenna studied her determined face before a bitter tightness began to rise in her throat. 'I underestimated you. Don't you care that Royce is hurt?'

'At the moment I'm more concerned for my grandson. Royce can take care of himself.'

She was ruthless. And Jenna knew Royce had inherited some of it from her. 'How do you think

he'll feel, knowing he's raising his brother's son?'
she asked.

'Isn't that what you're doing? If you can, so
can he.'

If there was ever the possibility of having a
normal marriage, it was gone now. She cringed
when she remembered the way he had looked at
her. But was it better to have a sterile marriage
than no marriage at all? Jenna stared at her for
another moment, then let out a long defeated
sigh. 'All right. If he still wants to go through
with it, I'll marry him.'

Mrs Drummond smiled exultantly.

On the following Monday morning they were
married in a very quiet ceremony before a judge
who was an old friend of the family. At the same
time, Royce filed papers to formally adopt
Robbie. No family or friends were present and
Jenna told herself it didn't matter. She was doing
something she wasn't very proud of.

Silence filled the small confines of Royce's
silver Jaguar when they left the courthouse and
sped through the thinning traffic. Swallowing
uneasily, she looked at his handsome profile and a
small bubble of hysteria tried to slide past the
hurt constricting her chest. This stranger is my
husband, she thought. I'm Mrs Royce
Drummond now.

He hadn't spoken a word to her since he had left
her flat Friday night. Mrs Drummond made all the
arrangements and told her to be at the judge's
chambers at nine o'clock on Monday morning. She
met him in the corridor and together, without a
word, they went in and exhanged their vows.

He sat next to her now in a severe black suit, looking more grim and haggard than she had ever seen him. Deep lines grooved his mouth, his strong jaw was set, his smouldering grey eyes intent on the road ahead. He tossed his head to an arrogant angle and the cool breeze from his open window ruffled his shining black hair.

Jenna felt small beside him, her hands twisting miserably in her lap, creasing the simple lines of her soft ivory jersey dress. A few loose strands of hair fell across her eyes and when she brushed them back, more came undone. A look of chagrin crossed her face. Why couldn't it stay up today of all days? Her wedding day. She had wanted to look nice, but it was a messy mouse-coloured mop on her head. For all the notice Royce took of her appearance, she could have been bald!

The car purred to a stop in his reserved parking space outside his office building and he turned toward her with eyes as icy as winter skies. 'This is simply another working day as far as I'm concerned,' he said shortly, his lips thinning as if he controlled himself with difficulty. 'Nothing's changed now that we're married. When we're in the office, you're my secretary, nothing more. Only at home, in front of my family, will I consider you my wife.'

'Very well, sir.' The cold lift of her lips was meant to be a smile. She would begin as she meant to go on. Taking the wide gold band from her finger with a show of supreme indifference, she dropped it into her bag. 'Thank you for the lift.' She pushed on the door and walked quickly to the building, crushing back a swift rush of hurt. She shouldn't have expected anything else. It doesn't matter, she told herself. She wouldn't let it matter. This marriage was for Robbie's benefit, not hers.

Chad Redwicke was standing at the time clock when she punched in. 'A little late this morning, aren't you?' he sneered. 'And you said you handed in your resignation on Friday. Was it just a ploy to get the boss to notice you? A little too obvious, don't you think?'

She coldly pushed past him without answering.

'Don't ignore me when I talk to you, Iceberg!' He grabbed her arms and spun her around to face him, bringing her up against his tall body. To anyone passing by, it looked like an embrace. 'There's such an air of mystery about you. No one knows what you're hiding. Tell me your secrets,' he murmured close to her face.

Vibrating with anger, she grated, 'Let me go——'

'If you must do that sort of thing, Jennifer,' Royce cut in coldly from behind them, his eyes narrowing to icy grey pinpoints, 'would you mind doing it in a less public place?'

Her breath caught harshly in her throat and she jerked herself out of Chad's unresisting arms, resentment blazing briefly as she watched Royce disappear down the hall, nodding to several of his colleagues. 'Don't you ever touch me again, Chad!' she muttered angrily.

'What'll you do? Scream for help? Royce Drummond won't come to your rescue, that's for sure. And you two looked so cosy last Friday. What happened? Did he realise you weren't his type? Or did you turn him down once too often? I told you a plain girl like you shouldn't be so choosy.'

'Damn you! Leave me alone!' she cried.

His eyes widened and he threw his head back with a rich mocking laugh. 'Well, well, so you're not the cool little secretary always in control! There's fire under all that ice after all. Look at those eyes shooting blazing blue sparks at me, and your face all flushed with righteous indignation. Why, you're almost beautiful, Jenna!'

She turned her back on him and stalked away, trying to block out his mocking laughter and the curious glances and whispers of several girls passing in the hallway.

When she got to her office, Royce was standing at her desk thumbing through some papers. His wintry gaze touched her for a fleeting instant before he turned and started back to his own office. 'Bring your notebook for dictation,' he said coldly.

Heat stained her cheeks and a fiery resentment burned in her eyes as she slung her handbag into a bottom drawer, picked up her notepad and followed him.

His dictation was fast and several times his words were muttered, but she never asked him to slow down or speak up. He was angry, and after she had calmed down, she told herself he had every right to be. She crushed her resentment and filled her notepad, and little by little all her anger ebbed away. She was left with only an empty sadness that she had hurt him so badly without meaning to.

When he had finished, he reached in his shirt pocket and found a card with a phone number on it and slid it across his desk. 'Get me Moira DuMont at this number and make dinner reservations for two at the club tonight for eight-thirty. Oh, and send her a dozen white roses.'

The clipped orders sent a fiery wave of crimson heat to her face and unbearable pain flashed in her eyes before it was quickly masked. There was no way to hide her shaking hands when she jotted down the instructions. This was their wedding day! Royce didn't have to drive home the point that it meant nothing to him so cruelly.

'Will there be anything else, sir?' she said quietly, barely keeping her voice cool and impassive.

'Yes.' She lifted her chin and waited. 'Stay away from Chad Redwicke.'

Rage rose in her throat. A bitter galling pain ran through her like a hot poker. 'But it's all right for you to flaunt your women in front of me? Get them on the phone for you? Send them roses?'

'It's what you're paid for!'

Her breath stopped harshly and pain twisted across her face before she sank her teeth into her bottom lip. 'How could I forget?' she choked. Rigid pride demanded that she walk quickly away so he wouldn't see her complete loss of composure.

Royce left the office early that morning, and with his customary inconsiderateness, he didn't tell her where he was going or when he'd be back.

I shouldn't have expected anything different, Jenna told herself when he still hadn't put in an appearance by five o'clock. It was just another working day.

The line at the time clock was long and several

girls stopped their chattering to give her sidelong
looks and curious stares, but Jenna didn't notice
them. She waited her turn without a word, then
punched out and ran to catch the bus. It was
crowded, but she didn't notice that either.
Everything passed in front of her in a blur—
faces, voices, blaring traffic. Nothing could touch
her on this warm spring afternoon with a hint of
summer in it. She had put her feelings in cold
storage. It didn't matter that this was her
wedding day and she was a June bride. She had
seen her husband for a total of twenty minutes
this morning and exhanged only half a dozen
words with him. She forced herself to remember
being Mrs Royce Drummond was simply another
job she was handsomely paid to do. A small smile
curved her mouth. Should she shock him and try
to be a paragon of a wife too? The thought was so
ludicrous her smile turned to a grin, and by the
time she started up the walk to Kate's house to
pick up Robbie, she had talked herself into good
spirits.

Kate met her at the door, her face wreathed in
smiles. 'It's finally happened!' she shouted, not
giving Jenna a chance to say hello. As she hugged
her tightly, Kate's happiness bubbled over and
became infectious. 'The agency's found a baby
for us! We get her tomorrow!'

'Oh, how wonderful! Congratulations!' Jenna
grinned. 'You'll make a great mother. I knew it
right away.'

'You always know the right thing to say.'
Kate's eyes sparkled as she dragged Jenna into
the house. 'Frank's just as thrilled as I am.'

At the mention of her husband's name, he got

up from the floor where he was playing with Robbie. Tall and thin and slightly balding, he wiped his hand down the side of his jeans, then held it out to Jenna. 'Glad to meet you. I've heard so much about you from Kate. This is quite a boy you've got here.'

'Thank you, and congratulations on your new daughter.'

He nodded, smiling. 'Sit down, won't you? Kate's been waiting for you to come so she could break out the champagne.'

'Here it is,' said Kate, coming from the kitchen, waving a big green bottle. 'Dom Perignon it's not, but I wouldn't know good from bad, so it'll have to do.'

'I've never tasted champagne,' Jenna said shyly, 'so I wouldn't know either.'

The plastic cork made a loud pop and hit the ceiling, and they all laughed as Frank made a big production out of pouring it into three mismatched stemmed water goblets and a tiny plastic mug with Bugs Bunny on it for Robbie.

'A little taste won't hurt him,' he said with a swagger.

Jenna pulled her son on to her lap and then they all held their glasses up to each other.

'To families,' said Frank.

'To babies who make families complete,' Kate said softly.

'To you and your new daughter. May you always be happy,' Jenna added.

'Hey, this is good stuff,' Frank marvelled.

'I hoped it would be. The only other time I had champagne was at our wedding.' Stars were shining in Kate's eyes. 'It's only right, isn't it, champagne at our wedding and now at the birth of our daughter?'

He nodded serenely and just for a moment Jenna envied their closeness. Pain flashed in her eyes but was instantly crushed.

Robbie took a drink and spat it down the front of his shirt before letting out a loud wail.

'Never mind, darling,' she laughed, drinking deeply and hugging him. 'It's probably an acquired taste.'

They all laughed, and for the first time that day Jenna relaxed and let the warm glow of good friends and cheap champagne melt the ice choking her heart.

It was seven-thirty before she went home. She had the taxi drop her at the open gate and she savoured the peaceful dusk as she shifted Robbie in her arms and started up the long circular drive.

Her legs felt wobbly and she knew she shouldn't have had so much to drink on an empty stomach, but she justified her actions by telling herself such a day came only once in a lifetime. Her lifetime, anyway. She had married the man she loved. She had a son to call her own and her friends were about to have a daughter. She really did have it all!

She twirled Robbie around and grinned up at the darkening sky, remembering Kate's surprise when the opportunity had presented itself and she had told her she was moving into the Drummond household.

Frank had patted her shoulder and refilled her glass, smiling fatuously, almost like father of the bride. 'We should have got a bigger bottle with all the things we have to celebrate.

Congratulations to you and Robbie, Jenna. I hope we'll still get to see you and this handsome hunk now and then.'

'Of course you will,' she assured him. 'I may be starting a new life in a rarefied atmosphere now, but I'll never forget my friends.'

'I'm so glad you've found love at last,' Kate grinned.

Jenna clinked her glass with theirs and laughed, but underneath it all, she knew love hadn't found her.

CHAPTER EIGHT

THE house at the end of the drive was huge, and with each step she took Jenna felt herself getting smaller and smaller. Royce never told her his home was actually a thirty-acre estate of woods, lawns and gardens overlooking Lake Ontario from the impressive Scarborough Bluffs. The house itself was a thirty-five-room grey brick mansion, and it was all Jenna could do to force herself to continue walking towards it.

Holding Robbie tightly in her arms, she had just stepped on to a shallow step at the bottom of the deep pillared portico when the massive double doors burst open and Adam came bounding out to meet her.

'Jennifer! Where have you been? Everybody's been waiting for you. Royce is frantic!'

She drew back, slightly dazed, and blinked up at him. 'Hello, Adam. Or is it Zachary? I've been collecting your nephew.' Her voice was husky, the words slurred, all at once she hiccupped.

'I'm Adam——'

There was a sudden commotion behind him, hurrying footsteps and loud exclamations as Jenna smiled up at Mrs Drummond and the rest of her children crowding behind her.

'Are you all right?' her mother-in-law asked, rushing down the shallow steps. 'You're so flushed. Royce missed you at the office, and when it got so late we thought you might have had an accident.'

Robbie was taken from her arms, but before Jenna could say a word, a car screeched to a halt behind her. As she turned, Royce slid from behind the wheel and strode angrily to them.

'Where have you been?' he snapped. His dark suitcoat was hanging open and his tie was undone and his shirt unbuttoned part way down. His hair stood on end as if he'd been dragging his hands through it.

Jenna blinked at him in surprise, swaying a little. Everything suddenly started to spin and she tried to find her voice, but nothing would come out. She hiccupped and cleared her throat and tried again. 'Hello, Royce. Were you looking for me? I was celebrating with Kate. I thought you were celebrating with——' Her forehead wrinkled. 'Isn't it Moira something-or-other this week?'

His eyes narrowed to molten slits. 'Good God, you're drunk!'

'I had two glasses of champagne.' She put a dazed hand to her face and swayed. Her hair slipped out of its coil and fell in her eyes. Trying to look away from the suddenly accusing faces of her new family, she felt defenceless and lost. 'That's not enough to make anybody drunk, is it?' She looked anxiously to the ground at her feet. 'Where's Robbie?'

'Susan took him into the house,' Royce said harshly, 'and that's where you're going right now.' Gesturing to the others to precede them, he took her arm and aimed her in the direction of the doorway, but she lost her balance and fell heavily against him. 'Two glasses of champagne!' he muttered between his teeth. Putting an arm around her and the other at her knees, he swept her up against his chest with a total disregard for her dignity.

'You're carrying me over the threshold,' she murmured, 'just like a real bride and groom. But we're not. You couldn't have made that very clear to the rest of your family, by the way they were acting.'

'Just shut up, Jennifer. I've been half out of my mind wondering what happened to you and you waltz in here drunk. *Drunk!* How could you?'

'I couldn't very well refuse to celebrate with Kate. They're getting a daughter tomorrow. They'll be a real family now. Besides, I'd never tasted champagne before.' She stared at him before letting her hand settle on the back of his neck where his hair clung lovingly to her fingers. It was the most natural thing in the world to let them trail over his ears in a featherlight caress. 'You have nice ears.'

He jerked his head roughly away from her. 'Don't!'

'You're ticklish,' she marvelled. 'Your handsome ears are ticklish.' Her laugh was soft and husky.

She was dimly aware of being carried up some stairs. High ceilings flashed by and she caught sight of an ornate wall sconce and oil paintings in wide gilt frames and deep thick carpeting. At least she thought there must be carpeting. Royce's steps didn't make any sound, and that was strange considering the quick way he was moving.

She let her eyes close, giving herself up to the floating sensation. How nice to be here, safe,

secure, cradled against the warm muscular wall of
his chest. She could hear the slow drumming of
his heart and wished time would stop so she
could stay like this for ever.

'I love you, you know,' she murmured,
slipping a hand inside his unbuttoned shirt and
blinking artlessly wide blue eyes up at him. Her
hair spilled over his arm in a heavy brown mass.

His step faltered for a split second, then his lips
tightened to a thin grim line.

'I'm sorry I'm not beautiful like your other
women. It isn't fair for such a handsome man to
have such a plain wife. You should have had Meg
or—— I thought you were having dinner with
Moira DuMont tonight?' Her forehead wrinkled
as if she should remember something, but then
she shrugged. 'Moira—that's such a classy name,
isn't it? I'll bet she's beautiful, too.' A small sigh
escaped her. 'Meg always said I had a face that
would stop a clock.' Her fingers unconsciously
curled into his warm moist skin.

'Meg doesn't know what she's talking about,'
Royce muttered, pushing open a door at the end
of the hall and unceremoniously dropping her to
her feet.

She would have fallen if he hadn't put both
hands out to steady her.

'Have you had anything to eat today?' he asked,
roughly removing her hand from inside his shirt
as if it irritated him.

Her head spun when she tried to remember. 'I
was too nervous this morning. And too busy at
lunchtime.' She brushed her hair out of her
dazed eyes. 'You wouldn't believe how many
people were asking for you today. Kate was going

to send out for some Chinese food, but I had to get Robbie home——' She looked away from his grim face and suddenly noticed she was in a bedroom. 'I can't go to bed until I've seen to Robbie.'

'Never mind. Mother and Susan will take care of him. They're perfectly capable.'

Jenna swallowed convulsively. 'I should be there. He'll probably feel strange. What if he cries for me? Or starts that choking cough?'

'They'll know what to do. Right now you're in no condition to even take care of yourself.'

'I'm perfectly capable. After all, I'm a paragon, aren't I?' She smiled at him, a dazzling smile full of promise.

Royce's look of irritation changed to a curious bleakness mingled with pain. 'I was wrong to think you could handle this. When I found out about you and Peter I should have called the whole thing off. Did the thought of having to marry his brother terrify you so much you had to get drunk before you could come to me?'

Jenna's whole face changed. Her eyes widened and became a brilliant bottomless blue. 'Peter has nothing to do with it. When everything was said and done, I married you because I love you. I always have.'

His hands tightened on her arms and brought her up sharply against him. 'Do you know what you're saying?'

'Of course,' she exclaimed indignantly, her words only slightly slurred. 'Every ounce of sense I have tells me I shouldn't, but I can't help it. You despise me, but I love you. You didn't really think I was any different from all your other women, did you? I've wanted so desperately to be your wife, to have the right to be near you always.'

'Why do you have to say these things now?' Royce muttered, his mouth twisting as his fury fled, leaving him an empty ache in its place. 'You're only complicating things. You're not supposed to love me. You know I don't love you.'

'It doesn't matter.' She looked into strangely shimmering grey eyes. Oh, but it did matter! She wished just once he could look at her the way he looked at his other women. Her throat ached with unspoken pleading and every nerve throbbed with a painful, yearning hunger. 'If only I was beautiful——'

'Don't look at me like that,' he said in a savage undertone. 'You're so full of invitation, but you won't remember any of it in the morning.'

She watched the shape of his lips move as if in a wondrous, enchanted dream. Then she was floating to him, her body featherlight, warm and soft as she melted in his arms, arching herself against him with a sensuous languor that came to her as naturally as breathing.

He tried to thrust her away from him, but she clung with a surprising strength.

'Don't shut me out, Royce. Just this once, pretend I'm a beautiful woman.'

A look of torment crossed his face and with a long sigh of exasperation he bent his head towards her and brushed his lips lightly against hers. 'Goodnight, Jennifer. You'll thank me in the morning for not taking advantage of you.' He pried her soft body away from him.

But she couldn't let it end there. Both her

hands went up to frame his handsome face, dragging it down to hers, holding him still while she stood on tiptoe and pressed a demanding kiss to his mouth. When there was no answering return, she daringly ran the tip of her tongue across his lips and felt a betraying quiver run through him.

She was lost when his mouth opened warmly, covering hers, and with a sound that was almost a groan, his arms came right around her, crushing her to him.

Her head swam. She was conscious of the hard shuddering length of his body and the curious way his arms could be both gentle and rough at the same time. A wondrous thought came to her that her body was made for his. So small and slender, she melted into his tall, deceptive leanness. His mouth was fierce and achingly possessive, and whatever response he demanded, her untutored emotions answered, and the more he gave, the more she craved.

'I love you,' she murmured mindlessly into his mouth. 'I've been waiting for you all my life.'

His hands no longer bruised but roamed over her with gentle sensuality, and she gasped at the sudden sharpening of every one of her senses.

For an instant she drew back and looked straight into his face and saw so clearly all the strong angles and planes that made him so striking: thick black winged brows, grey eyes that were warm and caressing and unexpectedly gentle, the sharp straight line of his nose, the sensuous curve of his lips with the deep grooves on either side of them and the deep indentation in the middle of his chin.

She could feel the rapid thudding of his heart beneath her hands when she slid them from his neck inside his shirt, helplessly curling into the smooth muscled hardness of his chest. The faintly musky scent of his skin enveloped her and she breathed deeply, hearing his raw groan of desire before his mouth once again took hungry possession of hers, softening, deepening, giving her a taste of paradise.

A dazzling light danced before her eyes, bursting into a dizzy, spinning, blinding brilliance. Her head fell back, exposing the delicate creamy arch of her neck to his feverishly questing lips. Her yearning for him grew and became an agony. His hands burned through the slippery fabric of her dress, fiercely closing over her breasts.

Moving restlessly against her, his hands slid down to her hips, crushing her more firmly to him, and for the first time in her life Jenna felt the fullness of a man's desire.

Her eyes widened. She became rigid. Her heart rose in her throat and cold reason returned like a slap in the face. Just as quickly, her stomach began to churn sickeningly. 'Royce!' she muttered.

He felt her stiffen and drew slightly away so he could look at her. There was a glazed, burning look in his eyes and his hair curled damply across his forehead. 'What—Oh God!'

In a split second he turned and half dragged, half carried her to the bathroom, where she retched miserably before thoroughly disgracing herself all over her dress and his suit and the floor . . .

The sun slanted in long rays across the pale green carpet when Jenna woke the next morning. She turned over groggily, automatically reaching out to the table beside the bed for her alarm clock, wondering why it hadn't rung. But the table wasn't there. Her hand encountered empty air. Something was banging abominably in her head, and panic began to tremble through her. Why hadn't Robbie cried and roused her? He never slept late. She blinked bewilderedly, trying to get her bearings. Unfamiliar pale green walls stared at her and long wide windows with ivory silk draperies met her gaze. Sitting bolt upright, she couldn't understand where she was.

And then, feeling a sudden chill, she looked down at herself and gasped. She was stark naked! Huddling back on to her pillows, she clutched the blanket to her chin, trying to remember what happened. Her head throbbed miserably. She must remember.

'Such an attack of modesty!' a deep familiar voice murmured.

Her whole body jerked wildly before she turned and looked to the other side of the wide bed and saw Royce. He was lying perfectly at ease beneath the covers, looking disgustingly well rested. One tanned arm was behind his head and his black hair was rumpled. A day's growth of beard darkened his face.

'What's the matter?' he asked. 'You look as if this is a new experience for you.'

Jenna closed her eyes and breathed deeply, counting to ten. This had to be some hideous nightmare. This couldn't be happening. Not to her!

When she opened them again he was still there. 'How——? Did you and I——? Did we——?' She shuddered, her face flaming.

'Don't you remember?' He turned on his side and faced her, propping himself up on one elbow.

The blanket fell away from him and she noticed he didn't have a shirt on. For one horrified instant she wondered if he, too, was naked. Her heart bounded to her throat and she would have bolted out of bed, but without anything to cover her, she was trapped.

His smile was knowing. 'Well and truly caught, aren't you?'

'Please, Royce! What happened? Why are we sharing this bed?'

'Don't you remember?' His smile became maddening. 'Tell me just exactly what you do recall about last night.'

Jenna swallowed nervously. 'I remember walking towards your house. It looked so . . . so huge. And then your family was there. So many people . . . And then . . .' she moistened suddenly dry lips, '. . . and then I was sick.'

'That's it?'

'What else is there?' she barely whispered. The sound was full of dread.

'You don't remember throwing yourself into my arms and telling me you loved me?'

All the colour drained from her face.

'Don't look so stricken. I knew it was the alcohol talking. Some people get belligerent when they drink. Some weep. Some giggle. You got all soft and loving, tantalising me with an air of sweet promise.'

She shrank back into the pillows and wanted to die. Her teeth bit sharply into her bottom lip to hold back a trembling sob of despair. 'That must have given you a good laugh!'

'You were different from what I expected, I'll give you that,' he said softly. 'I've caught glimpses of your passion before and had to wonder what the real Jennifer Caldwell was like. For someone who projects the image of untouchable ice, you're really something.'

Almost automatically Jenna lifted her chin, determined not to cower in front of him. However much she dreaded the answer, she had to know. 'Was it your idea or mine that we— sleep—here together?'

With slow deliberate movements, Royce closed the wide space separating them. His big warm hand reached out to stroke her cheek before sliding down to rest on the side of her neck, making her shiver. 'You're my wife,' he whispered huskily, a muscle jerking in his jaw. 'Last night was our wedding night. Why shouldn't we sleep together?'

Unexpected pain flashed in her eyes. She had slept with him and she had missed it! Shouldn't she have remembered something as momentous as that? Shouldn't she feel differently now? More complete somehow? But all she felt was bewildered panic. 'You said it would be a platonic relationship,' she choked.

'You changed the conditions of our marriage, not I,' Royce murmured thickly.

'Oh, God,' she muttered, wishing she could move away from him but afraid that one false move would dislodge the blankets and bring down even more humiliation on her.

So now he must know she wasn't Robbie's real
mother. Why wasn't he asking a million questions? Instead, she was full of them. What
actually happened between them? Her knowledge
of the intimacies shared by husbands and wives
was limited to biology books and romance novels
that hinted at all sorts of things but never really
told her much. If only she could remember!
Had it been good? Did he enjoy it? Did she do
it right? Had she made him happy? But how
could she come right out and ask him such
things? She was becoming more and more
intensely aware of the nearness of his lean hard
body and slightly musky scent, and she began
to quiver and her cheeks stung with a brilliant
heated colour.

His fingers curled on her neck, caressing the
slender bones, not letting her move. A flash of
pain ran across Royce's face as if he remembered
something he'd rather forget. Just for an
instant, he looked so vulnerable, but then it
vanished.

Her heart plunged and a freezing coldness
swept over her. Faltering under his penetrating
gaze, she tried to keep her composure in spite of
the stinging shame and embarrassment coursing
through her. It could not have been very good.
He must have been turned off by her inexperi-
ence.

'There's no excuse for what I did last night,'
she said huskily. 'Saying I'm sorry won't change
anything. But if you're waiting for an explanation,
I can't give you one. I can't even begin to try to
make you understand.'

Royce studied her and a strange light flickered across his face before his lips twisted with icy displeasure. He moved his hand away as if she contaminated him. 'You've got more stubborn pride than anybody I've ever known! What are you ashamed of? Getting drunk? Or making love to me?' Scorn dripped from his voice. 'You don't remember, do you?' he grated angrily.

Her breathing stopped. Her eyes became huge and stricken.

'The most passionate woman I've ever held in my arms and you don't remember!' He kept staring at her, the blanket the only thing between them. He was breathing hard and the air was heavy with something she couldn't understand. Then he levered himself away from her and moved to the other side of the bed with a sound of disgust rumbling deep in his throat. 'Don't worry. In spite of your tantalising act of incredible innocence and smouldering passion, I couldn't forget my brother had you first. I've never taken his leavings before, and I'm not about to start now. The only reason we shared this bed is because Adam kept hanging around wanting to make sure you were all right. I think it'll put his mind at rest if he believes we're a normal married couple for a while.'

'But——'

His look of freezing scorn silenced her. 'For the rest of the week, until my mother gets married on Saturday, I'll be sleeping here. This bed is wide enough to sleep four comfortably. You won't even know I'm here.'

Jenna made a helpless movement beneath the blankets. Even if he was on the other side of this huge house, she'd be conscious of his every move.

'You don't have to be full of regrets, Jennifer. I've got enough for both of us.' He stood up, and she was thankful to see the black silk of his pyjama bottoms. 'When you threw up last night, you ruined your dress and my suit,' he said harshly. 'Before you passed out I undressed you.'

At her gasp of embarrassment, his mouth twisted derisively. 'You were quite willing, and in different circumstances I might have enjoyed it. Your things are in the closet.' He gestured to two louvred doors on the wall behind him. 'Everything is there. I took the liberty of moving all your belongings yesterday. That's how I spent my time, in case you wondered. Your landlady was grateful she didn't have to evict you as she threatened.'

Her head shot up automatically and she opened her mouth to say something, but he sliced through her denial.

'Don't bother denying it. She took great pleasure in showing me the eviction notice.'

Jenna's chin dipped back down to her chest in defeated silence. There was nothing she could say. It was useless even to try.

'If only you'd waited a few more minutes before leaving the office . . .' The thin thread of anger ran out of him, leaving his voice curiously raw and full of pain. 'I didn't expect you to have to find your own way home. My mother had arranged a small reception for us with my family and a few close friends, but when I got back to the office, my paragon of independence had already gone.'

She looked up quickly, confusion making her frown. 'But—I thought you had a date with Moira DuMont? I made reservations——'

'You have a pretty low opinion of me, don't you? It was our wedding day, Jennifer.'

'But—the white roses you had me send——'

'I send roses to a lot of different women for a lot of different reasons. You're my wife now, but that doesn't mean I have to start explaining my actions to you.'

She stared in bewilderment. 'Then, all along, you didn't intend to have dinner with another woman just to humiliate me?'

His lip curled. 'Well, I guess I know where I stand with you, don't I?' His jaw hardened. 'No, Jennifer, I didn't intend to humiliate you. You do it easily enough all by yourself. Moira DuMont is a client and the reservation was for her and Bill Hallor, the vice-president of our company, in case you've forgotten him. That's the only explanation you'll get from me—and it's the last time I make one.'

Her heart lurched with a pang of regret. Yesterday could have been beautiful if only she hadn't misjudged him so completely. How many other times had she done the same thing? The silence stood between them, thinning, lengthening, and then her voice faltered, 'I'm sorry——'

'I'm sorry too, Jennifer, more than you'll ever know.' Royce sighed, running a hand through his hair, then straightened his shoulders and lifted his head with resigned acceptance. 'Now I suggest you get up and get dressed and go downstairs to see how our son is doing. I don't expect you at the office today. You'll have enough to do just trying to settle Robbie in here.'

As she watched him walk away, she knew the gap between them had widened to a deep yawning chasm of misunderstanding. If only she hadn't jumped to conclusions. If only she hadn't been so ready to believe the worst of him. If only she hadn't been so blindly, stubbornly proud . . .

CHAPTER NINE

When Jenna left the bedroom, everything was hushed and still along the upper hallway. A mixture of awe and trepidation made her steps falter as she started down the curving staircase. How was she going to apologise to her new family without making more of a fool of herself? Her feet sank noiselessly into the oyster shell carpeting centred on each wide step of pale, gold-veined marble. She gulped nervously, brushing sweaty hands down the sides of her simple blue cotton dress, forcing herself to keep moving.

There was a dull ache behind her eyes, but that was the least of her worries. With each step she took, she lost a little more of her self-containment. This house was in a world far removed from her. With her imagination working overtime, she pictured all the other women in the Drummond family who had descended this staircase in the past, and something inside her shrivelled. What was she doing here? She was out of her depth. She was plain and gauche and awkwardly inexperienced. Tension was written all over her as she hesitated nervously on the bottom stair.

The front hall was round and vast, with a sparkling crystal chandelier dripping from the ceiling on a gossamer thin gold cable, the late morning sun striking its prisms to cast rainbow puddles on the shining marble floor.

Several open doorways led in different directions and to her left, she glimpsed a huge room filled with golden sunshine and elegant chairs and sofas and tables arranged in comfortable groups around a commanding marble fireplace. A gold-toned Oriental rug was on the floor and slim, green-gold drapes with matching valances at the tall windows. On the far side of the room were French doors opening on to a stone terrace and beyond that to a rose garden in full bloom.

The room was empty now, but she pictured the people who most probably had been in here last night: gorgeous women in costly gowns sipping sherry, handsome men in velvet dinner jackets drinking—what? She was so unrefined she didn't even know what men drank in the evenings. She was sure it wasn't the beer her father preferred when he was alive.

'Hi, Jennifer,' a bubbly voice behind her broke into her thoughts, scattering them in a thousand different directions. 'I'm Susan. I don't expect you remember me from last night?'

She turned stiffly, taking a deep breath in an effort to find an aloof composure. But the sight of Royce's sister shattered it at once and she felt herself gaping.

Susan was tall and slender, with a short cap of curly black hair hugging her face, and her bright blue eyes were sparkling with mischief. She wore a disreputable pair of jeans and a blazing red T-shirt and her laugh was rich and full. 'I can't thank you enough for marrying Royce,' she said, coming straight to the point. 'I know you were forced into it, but we just couldn't let someone as down-to-earth as you are get away!'

Jenna kept staring, incredulously. She had expected Royce's sister to be a younger version of her mother and just as sophisticated, but Susan's open, friendly manner completely threw her. She was a very young, unaffected seventeen-year-old whose welcome was warm and genuine.

'We were so afraid he'd marry some fashion-plate who'd expect us to be formal all the time and drape herself in mink and diamonds and want to be waited on hand and foot and eat caviar and drink champagne all day. When Royce began telling us about this paragon of a secretary he had, who was just as ordinary as we are, I'm afraid we badgered him into proposing. Forgive us, will you?' She blinked brightly, not at all contrite. 'You won't have to lift a finger. We'll do everything we can to show our gratitude.' She dropped a sisterly arm on Jenna's shoulders, turning her towards the French doors. 'Mother's out here with Robbie. Oh, it's so good to have a baby around the house!'

Jenna was at a loss. Her head was spinning with the generosity of her sister-in-law. Not one word of reproach had been uttered. She was chattering away, making Jenna feel at ease and at home. It was so different from what she had anticipated.

'Ah, there you are, girls.' Mrs Drummond was sitting on a wrought iron patio chair with Robbie in her lap as they stepped on to the terrace. 'Robbie and I have been getting acquainted.' She smiled warmly, hugging him before handing him to Jenna.

He gurgled contentedly in his grandmother's arms, and Jenna felt a sudden rush of moisture sting her eyes. 'Mrs Drummond, about last night . . .'

'Now, now, you don't have to explain a thing.' She waved away the attempt at an apology. 'And don't go feeling embarrassed either, my dear. Royce explained it all. It's the most natural thing in the world to be sick if you're too nervous to eat anything all day long. We're just glad you're all right this morning. And do call me Olivia. We're family now.'

'Tell her about Robbie spitting up all over Royce,' Susan laughed, wrinkling her nose at the baby and making him giggle.

A smug, satisfied look crossed Mrs Drummond's face. 'That was the best thing that could have happened. Susan had just finished bathing Robbie and asked Royce to hold him while she went for his diapers.' Her smile widened to a grin. 'And just as he took him, Robbie lost his dinner all over Royce's shirt.'

'Oh no!' Jenna could just imagine his reaction.

'I wish you could have seen it,' Susan laughed, enjoying it again in the telling. 'For one shocked instant he just stood there. Then he started laughing so hard tears rolled down his face. He said you'd done the same thing to him barely fifteen minutes before and maybe it was some kind of omen!'

Jenna wanted to die of embarrassment, but Mrs Drummond was laughing so hard, she had to smile.

'That's not all,' Susan chuckled. 'He turned right around and insisted on bathing Robbie again—all by himself! And he even took his temperature to make sure there was nothing more wrong with him than just an upset stomach.'

Jenna stood stock still, her eyes widening with wonder. She never would have believed it of Royce. All her preconceived ideas about her playboy employer—her playboy husband—were not proving true.

Mrs Drummond must have seen her scepticism turn to bewilderment and she rubbed her hands together. 'Now he's had a taste of being a real father! I knew you'd be good for him, Jennifer.' She got to her feet briskly and started into the house. 'Come along, dear. We'll show you what we've done to accommodate Robbie and then see about getting you some breakfast. I imagine you're hungry by now. Royce has already gone to the office and told me he's given you the day off. I've made some plans for us this afternoon if you're feeling up to it.'

Her matter-of-fact briskness was soothing and put Jenna at ease, and she was content to follow wherever she led, trying not to make a fool of herself by gaping too much at the magnificent rooms.

'I don't doubt that you'll feel a bit overwhelmed at first,' she said gently, 'but I want you to remember one thing: this is a home first, a house second. There are things here, some costly, some merely beautiful and kept for sentimental reasons, but it's the people here who are most important. If you never lose sight of that fact, my dear, you'll be all right.'

'You've been so kind to me, Mrs Drummond— all of you have—I don't deserve it.'

'My dear, you must try to get over that feeling

of selfconsciousness and inferiority. We're no different than any other of your friends. It just won't do any more. You've got to realise you're Mrs Royce Drummond now, and that's quite a feather in our caps, believe me. When I think of some of the women I've seen him with . . .' She shuddered delicately. 'Anyway, will you put yourself in my hands for the next few hours?'

Jenna's voice was soft and shy. 'I can learn so much from you, Mrs—Olivia. I'd be foolish to refuse.'

If she had realised what her mother-in-law had in mind, her pride would have forced her to refuse. Expecting to be introduced to the housekeeper, Mrs MacPherson, and the other daily help she had noticed on her swift tour or perhaps lectured on how to keep such a huge home running smoothly, she was shocked when, instead, Adam, Zachary, Ryan and Susan burst into the breakfast room and announced that since Jenna had finished eating, the chauffeur was ready any time she was.

Mrs Drummond ignored Jenna's questioning frown and smiled at her children. 'You've made all the arrangements, then?'

Susan nodded, mischief dancing in her eyes. 'Don't worry about Robbie this afternoon. He'll be in good hands.'

'Are we going somewhere?' she asked quietly, surprised but at the same time wary.

'Mother won't tell you,' Adam teased. 'It's a surprise.'

'But——'

'And don't let the idea of a chauffeur bother you,' Susan laughed. 'That was Ryan's touch. He has a friend whose father runs a limousine service and he talked him into putting on a uniform and running you downtown. I haven't got my driver's licence yet and we didn't want you to have to take the bus. Next month, though, I'll drive you anywhere!'

Ryan blushed when Jenna thanked him. 'I'm still trying to be charming,' he said sheepishly.

'You are, every one of you.' Her smile was warm as she followed her mother-in-law out to the car.

But when they reached their destination, Jenna was chagrined. 'Mrs Drummond, I know you mean well, but——'

'You've put yourself in my hands, remember?' She cut off her objections and forced her into the exclusive little beauty salon. 'We won't hear any more about it. Trust me to know what I'm doing.' She turned to the owner of the salon who obviously had been waiting for them. 'Well, Antoine, here she is. What do you think?' She kept a heavy hand on Jenna's shoulder, silently commanding her to stand still.

The tall man with a very pronounced French accent stood looking at Jenna critically, pursing his lips, lifting her hair. Then he smiled. 'We will make her beautiful!'

Mrs Drummond nodded her assent. 'If anyone can bring out her good points, it's you, Antoine, Jennifer has grown up in the shadow of a glamorous sister, so she doesn't think there's anything there. I trust you'll convince her?'

'Ah.' His voice was laced with gentle sympathy. 'Just leave everything to me.'

'I have some shopping to do while you're with

Antoine, my dear,' she turned briskly to Jenna. 'I'd listen to him if I were you. He's the best in the business.'

For the next several hours Jenna was introduced to a world she had only heard about before. Antoine kept up a steady flow of encouragement, beginning with suggestions of hairstyles to suit her facial shape. Sometimes he did the work himself, with much hand-waving and busily snipping scissors, and sometimes he handed her over to one of his assistants. Asking her opinions, he weighed them objectively. He knew something of her lifestyle and offered his considerable wisdom, but always let the final decision be her own.

Finally cut to a more managable length, her hair was then lightly permed so soft waves would flatter her face and tumble about her shoulders. A conditioning rinse brought out dark red highlights she hadn't known were there. Her nails were manicured, her eyebrows plucked to a delicate arch, and she was taught how to use a contouring make-up base, eyeshadow, mascara, blusher and lipstick.

But throughout the long afternoon, she didn't enjoy herself. She kept picturing her handsome husband and knew, no matter what she might try, she'd never be able to compete with the truly beautiful women in his life. This was all artifice. She was still the same person underneath.

When they were finally done, Jenna caught sight of herself in a mirror and stared for long silent seconds. The woman staring back had eyes wide and brilliantly blue framed by thick dark lashes. Her skin was flawless, a translucent ivory oval surrounded by reddish-brown waves. Stepping closer to the mirror, she put out a tentative hand and touched the cool glass. 'It's really me!' she whispered, stunned, her heart expanding.

Antone blinked brightly. 'So many women have been conditioned to believe they are not beautiful. All it takes is knowing how to make the most of what you have and someone to believe in you.'

She turned artlessly, looking him straight in the eye. 'Am I beautiful?'

'You can see for yourself, Mrs Drummond. Mirrors don't lie.'

Jenna looked back at herself and all at once her lips began to curve in a radiant smile. 'I am. Oh, I am!'

He chuckled. 'This is but the beginning for you. Now you must find the confidence within yourself to continue. Beauty is more than a pretty face—it's a feeling. If you believe in yourself, value yourself, project a positive attitude, people will naturally be attracted to you. Come, we will find your mother-in-law.'

Olivia Drummond's face was glowing when she saw her. 'I knew it!' she breathed reverently, staring for long seconds.

Warming to the praise, Jenna impulsively reached up and kissed her lightly on the cheek. 'How can I ever thank you?'

'Seeing Royce's reaction to such beautiful results will be thanks enough,' she beamed. 'He doesn't know how lucky he is.'

'That will be the real test, won't it?' she said softly, tingling with a mixture of anxiety and anticipation.

But Royce's reaction was totally unexpected.

Jenna was standing beside Robbie's cot in the small nursery off their bedroom when he came home from work. A faint sound interrupted the soft lullaby she crooned and, stiffening, she turned to see him coming towards her.

He had removed his jacket and tie and was unbuttoning his shirt when he stopped dead. His grey eyes were piercing when they rested on her deeply waving red-brown hair before skimming over her eyes with their thick, soot-smudged lashes and her flawless skin and faintly trembling mouth. She was wearing a new dress, an aquamarine vision of floating chiffon that hugged her tiny waist and whispered about her knees in soft folds.

Without a word, he came closer and looked straight into her face intently, for long disturbing seconds, before raking over her figure in the new and obviously expensive dress. Something flickered in his eyes, but he blinked it away at once. Then he threw his head back and laughed. *Laughed*, long and hard.

Jenna tried to look away, but he held her with his grim grey gaze so at variance with his mirthless laughter.

'Whose idea was it?' he asked roughly, his mouth becoming a bleak, thin, twisting line.

A hot wave of anger and mortification ran into her burning face. She started to turn, but he roughly gripped her chin with his strong fingers, raising it and forcing her to look straight into his eyes.

'What am I supposed to do? See what a gorgeous wife I've got at home and forget all the other women in the world?'

Unbearable hurt squeezed her heart before she gathered up her pride and stiffened the small length of her body. 'No, Royce. I know that's too much to ask. I did this for me, not for you.'

'I don't believe it. This had to be something my mother dreamed up to make me fall in love with you. She's such a romantic!' His tone was heavy with disgust. 'I thought you had more sense! She's wasting her time, and so are you.'

He didn't stay home for dinner that evening, much to the dismay of his family, and when he did come back much later, he moved his things with absolute finality to another bedroom on the opposite side of the house.

Adam became more openly protective after that, and Jenna expected her life to be untenable, but she was pleasantly surprised to find she was wrong. Whatever explanation Royce had made to his family, they accepted it and didn't interfere any more. Royce kept his distance and was indifferently polite to her both at home and in the office, and she found she could live with that.

The only really awkward moments were when she came upon him unexpectedly caring for Robbie. He seemed a different person then, young and gentle and almost carefree, and it disconcerted her.

Once, in the middle of the night, she thought she heard Robbie whimper softly. Instantly awake, she ran, stumbling, into the nursery and stopped dead when she saw Royce standing there in jeans and a flannel shirt, holding Robbie safely in his arms. She'd never seen him in anything but three-piece suits and ties and sports coats before. He suddenly looked so—so ordinary yet so vulnerable dressed this way, and she couldn't take her eyes off him.

'Just a bad dream, I think,' he said quietly, his face and voice gentle. 'I'm sorry he woke you. I tried to quiet him before he did.'

Jenna hovered in the doorway in a long white cotton nightgown, her feet bare, her hair a sleep-tangled mass on her shoulders. 'I thought I heard something, but I wasn't sure,' she gulped, not knowing whether to stay or retreat. It was a little late now to think about putting a robe on and she willed herself not to cross her arms protectively in front of her. He was her husband, after all. He had seen her in far less before.

Slow colour began to creep into her face as the seconds ticked by.

Royce regarded her in the stretching silence, his grim grey eyes fixed on her. Something came and went in them before he turned back to the baby now asleep in his arms. 'It's times like these that make me feel he's really mine,' he said in an oddly thick, almost choking voice.

It's the same for me, Jenna wanted to tell him. But she couldn't. Her lips shook and her throat closed up. She managed a strangled whisper: 'He's your son, Royce, as much as he's mine.'

His mouth twisted in a bleak travesty of a smile as he laid him back in his cot and gently tucked the covers about him. Then he looked up, the grimness in his eyes darkening. 'I don't think so, Jennifer.' Very slowly he turned and left her.

There were times, mostly at weekends, when she caught glimpses of him striding across the marble-smooth lawns or wandering through the rose garden with its stone fountain spouting water into a fishpond, sometimes talking with the gardener, sometimes merely enjoying the solitude of the spacious grounds, standing at the edge of the bluff with the deep blue water of Lake Ontario spread out below him, but always with Robbie firmly anchored in the crook of his arm.

Robbie was beginning to walk and talk now, and Jenna didn't know whether to be elated or chagrined when his first clear word was 'Daddy' and his first faltering steps were towards the man who had changed their lives so drastically.

Jenna watched from a distance and never intruded on these moments between father and son. The rest of the week was hers, because Royce never came home from work before midnight and was often gone at dawn. He kept his distance and she kept hers, and it worked out fairly well.

A deliriously happy Olivia was married and had been honeymooning in the Caribbean for a month when Meg returned from Italy and interrupted the quiet pattern of Jenna's comfortably ordered life.

It was nearly noon and Jenna had just finished typing a letter when her office door burst open dramatically. Meg stood there dripping with mink. Considering the soaring mid-July temperature outside, Jenna thought she looked ludicrous, but she kept her voice even.

'Meg! How good to see you again. You're looking gorgeous!'

'And you,' Meg said bitterly, her eyes hard and envious as they swept over Jenna's hair and face and slender figure in a white linen dress. 'Royce told me I wouldn't recognise you, and he was right.'

'Royce told you?' Jenna's smile faltered a little.

'He's been telling me a lot of things lately. I've had dinner with him every night this week.' Meg watched the colour slowly drain from her sister's face with malicious satisfaction. 'You didn't know that, did you? And I'm having lunch with him today. Didn't he tell you?'

Jenna looked quickly away, struggling to keep her face expressionless. 'Of course he did. I must have forgotten.'

'You didn't forget.' Meg advanced closer to the desk. 'Don't pretend with me. I know you, Jenna. He's seeing other women, isn't he? He's already tired of you. I told him before he married you it wouldn't work. You were stupid to think it would.'

A numbing coldness crept over her. 'Yes, I know.'

'He should have married me!'

'If you hadn't tampered with Robbie's birth certificate . . .'

Meg's laugh was mocking. 'Oh no, that was the smartest thing I ever did. That's why he despises you so much. Peter had you first! Isn't that rich?'

'Only you would appreciate the irony of it.' Jenna's heart seemed to shrivel. 'And you're not going to tell him what really happened, are you? How it was you instead of me?'

'And have him stop despising you? Oh no, Jenna. You're that kid's mother. He'll never hear any different from me.'

Jenna let out a bitter sigh, searching her face, trying to understand her. 'You hate me so much,

Meg. It makes you feel good to know I'm not happy. Why?'

Her sister's sneer was full of triumph. 'You thought you were so responsible. *You*, Jenna. What did you know about life? Mom was wrong to ask you. All you ever did was run things and tell me what not to do. I showed you, didn't I? I don't need you!'

Jenna took a deep calming breath. 'I didn't realise you saw my concern as interference.' All her anger left her. 'I'm sorry, Meg. If I had it to do over again, things would be different. I've changed since becoming part of the Drummond family. Now I know how it feels to be loved and accepted.'

'Royce only married you to give the kid a name. He doesn't love you. He didn't marry you for yourself!'

Jenna managed to keep her voice level. 'I know that, Meg. That's all there is between us. It's his family who loves me. I take care of them for him and in return, he provides for Robbie and me. It's a fair arrangement.'

'Are you telling me you don't mind sharing him with all those kids as well as who knows how many mistresses?' She just couldn't resist turning the knife. 'And I thought you were the one with all the pride!'

'You wouldn't understand.' Jenna was beginning to tremble and she folded her hands tightly in her lap, trying not to let it show.

'I'm not stupid, but you are. He's only using you.'

A miserable, wrenching pain twisted inside her as she turned her head away. 'I don't need you to tell me that.' Hot tears were gathering in her throat and it hurt to talk.

'Why, you love him! Plain Jenna Caldwell dares to love Royce Drummond!' Meg was genuinely shocked. 'How dare you?'

Taking great calming breaths, Jenna felt her fierce pride erupting, beginning to break through her icy control. 'How dare I? Do you think love is only for the beautiful? Do you think because I'm plain, I haven't got any feelings?' The blazing blue of her eyes was the only colour in her face. 'Yes, I love him, Meg. And that's something you don't know anything about. You only know how to use people. You take what they offer, but you don't know how to give. You've never given anything in your whole life!'

A loud sound of disgust came from Meg's throat. 'Ever the martyr, aren't you? Poor put-upon Jenna! It wasn't my fault you slaved away for me and I didn't appreciate it.' Her face changed. 'Come out of your dream world. There are no fairy godmothers to do away with your wicked sister. I want Royce and I'll have him. I could make him happy in a way you never could. Do you think he appreciates the way you're slaving for him? You're an embarrassment, that's all.'

Jenna drew an unsteady breath. 'What's wrong, Meg? You've only been married a little over a month yourself. Are you tired of Carlo already?'

'That peasant!' Meg said scathingly. 'He's not half as rich as he said he was. It's his father, the Borchini Cosmetic Company, who has all the money. He just gets an allowance.'

'I see.' Jenna's heart turned over in sympathy for the hapless Carlo. 'Didn't he know you didn't really want him, only his money?'

'I want Royce,' said Meg in a deadly quiet voice.

Jenna looked her straight in the eye for a long disturbing minute. 'I don't think he wants you,' she said just as quietly. 'He's my husband.'

'What happened to your pride? Let him go. Don't wait until he asks you to leave.'

'Oh no, Meg. He's not going to ask me.' Why should he? she thought. He's got it made. He can have all the women he wants, right under my nose, and I can't say a word. I have to pretend they don't even exist. It's what I'm being paid for.

'I'll make him leave you for me,' Meg said spitefully.

'I'm sure you aren't the first who's tried and you won't be the last.' Jenna's voice was cool and matter-of-fact. 'He may see a lot of different women, but I'm the one he married. You're not going to change that.'

'Just you watch me!'

And Jenna did watch her—for four long weeks. It was a struggle not to let her feelings show. Royce was looking more and more handsome every time Jenna saw him. A terrible yearning gnawed at her steadily. She found that love was a miserable emotion she could do without. But it only grew stronger and more tenacious with every attempt she made to crush it.

It was galling to think Royce cared so little for her feelings, but she was too proud and too stubborn to compete with her sister for him. In a way, she was grateful he didn't date Meg behind her back any more. Her imagination could be so much more vivid than the real thing.

Safely entrenched behind an icy mask of complete control, she made nightly reservations at expensive restaurants for them without a murmur and sent dozens of roses and ordered exquisite jewellery she knew would suit Meg's taste as well as her greed.

Several times in those weeks Royce came to her desk, staring at her, searching her face with his arms folded grimly, not saying a word. It was as if he was waiting for her to make some comment about Meg. But she would stare back calmly, disconcerting him.

One hot August afternoon he came into her office and was about to pass her desk without a glance when, for some reason, he stopped and looked at her in the sharp unbroken silence. She sat perfectly still and straight and watched him without expression.

'Nothing touches you, does it?' he said, standing with his face set in chilling lines, his lip curling with contempt. 'Not even your selfish sister.'

'You'd be surprised,' she said cryptically, deliberately ignoring the storm signals in his eyes, handing him a thick sheaf of papers. 'Chad Redwicke stopped in earlier and asked me to hand these to you personally.' Turning back to her typewriter, she tried to shut him out of her mind.

'Stay away from that wolf!' he grated, a hard flush slowly creeping up his neck. 'You're my wife!'

'Not in this office, I'm not.' Her voice was level but defiant and she looked at him with enormous cold blue eyes.

He swooped right around the desk then and roughly pulled open her bottom drawer. Her handbag was there, and she watched in bewildered fascination as he tore it open and sent the contents scattering all over her desk. 'Where is it?' he demanded.

'Where's what?'

'Your ring!'

Without stopping to think, Jenna jumped to her feet and quickly backed away from him, her hand creeping protectingly up to her throat.

'Ah!' He followed her, step by jerky step, his grey eyes glittering when he saw the thin gold chain on her neck. 'How good of you to wear it so close to your heart. I didn't know you cared.'

Gripping the chain in his powerful fist, he swiftly jerked it, snapping the fragile links and sending the ring sliding down into her bra. He began to laugh and she glared at him in helpless rage as he deftly trust his hand down the front of her dress, searching for it.

For one pulsing second he looked straight into her eyes and she couldn't control an involuntary shiver. All her defences suddenly splintered. Naked need and yearning sprang like a flame from her to him.

'Oh, God, Jenna——' His anger drained away.

She trembled violently. Both her hands clutched at his wrist, trying to still his suddenly restless fingers burning on the soft warm swell of her breasts.

'Don't!' she gasped.

'You're my wife,' he demanded raggedly.

'Not he——' The word was choked off by the sudden suffocating pressure of his mouth crushing hers. A swirling blackness ran before her eyes and she resisted him for one crazy moment then gave up the useless struggle. After all, it was what she wanted, what she craved. A dying little sob caught in her throat and her body instinctively arched towards his, melting against him. She was a boneless, quivering puppet, his to command. Her arms crept up to his neck and she caressed his head and sank her fingers into his thick black hair.

'Oh, Jenna,' he groaned against her mouth. 'Jenna——'

Surprising tears spilled helplessly from her eyes, rolling down her face, dampening his lips. She knew it wasn't love on his part. Later she would have to bear the sense of humiliation, knowing she should have been stronger and resisted him, but now, here, close to him like this, it didn't matter. Nothing mattered. She loved him, and for this moment he was hers.

'Jenna,' he murmured, suddenly tasting the salty tang of her tears, 'don't cry! Please don't cry!' He left her mouth and sought the pale length of her throat, his warm lips resting against her thickly pounding pulse. 'Things can't go on like this. I can't——'

She stiffened, trembling violently, then jerked herself away, staring at him, trying to read his twisted face. Was this the end, then? Had Meg finally succeeded?

Her tear-stained face held a trace of terror and Royce hurriedly slipped the ring on her finger, holding it there tightly, nearly crushing it. 'We have to talk, Jenna——'

A sudden cough behind them made them both start guiltily.

Chad Redwicke stood in the doorway. 'I did knock,' he said with a knowing saccharine smile.

Royce's whole body tensed before he turned. 'Haven't you ever heard of something called tact or discretion?' he muttered angrily, a faint hard flush creeping into his face. He ran his fingers over his hair to smooth it back into place.

Jenna's face flamed with guilty embarrassment as she swiftly checked the front of her dress and saw it gaping open.

'Oh, I started to leave,' Chad grinned, 'but then I stuck around to see if Jenna might need my help. I couldn't make up my mind if she was fighting you off or asking for it.'

'You're asking for it!' Royce snarled furiously, bristling at the derisive tone in Chad's voice.

Jenna watched Chad's smile become knowing and conspiratorial. 'You know how women are,' he chuckled, oblivious to the angry set of Royce's shoulders, the sudden curling of his fists, his wide bracing stance. 'Some plain women can't handle all the attention a new hairdo and make-up gives them. Jenna here thinks——'

Royce's fist shot out and Chad fell backwards on to the floor.

'Don't you ever say another word about my wife!' he shouted savagely. 'If you do, I'll beat you to a pulp! You won't have a tooth left in your head!'

'Your wife!' Chad's voice was thunderstruck. A thin trickle of blood came from his nose and his face was deathly white.

'That's right, my wife.' Royce grabbed Jenna's hand and held it up to show him the wide gold ring glinting on her finger.

'So that's why you changed so drastically!' Chad threw her a wounded look and struggled to his feet. 'I always wondered what deep dark secret you were hiding. You could have told me.'

'She doesn't have to answer to you. Now get out of here before I lose my temper and fire you!'

Chad opened his mouth to say something but evidently thought better of it. He snapped his jaw shut and walked out without another word.

Royce watched him go, then turned to Jenna. 'Get your things. We're going home where we can talk in private.'

'We can't,' she said shakily. Hope began to rise, but she made herself crush it, knowing it might lead to even more hurt. She was almost afraid to find out why he suddenly wanted it known that she was his wife. 'You've got a meeting with your accountant and then a dinner appointment with——' she leaned across her desk and searched her calendar, '—Sara Jennings.'

'Come with me, then. James makes my head spin with a lot of boring figures, but after the business is out of the way, the dinner is something we could enjoy together.'

A little quivering pain went through her. She stiffened her shoulders and faced him squarely. 'I'm sure I wouldn't enjoy it, Royce.' Her voice shook. 'Please let me keep at least a little of my self-respect. I don't want to meet your latest conquest.'

'Dammit, Jenna, she's not a conquest! She's a client. She's fifty-five years old and just inherited a dying publishing company from her husband. Someone told her a new line of advertising might help.

'Oh.' She stared at him, slow colour creeping up her neck, then guiltily looked away. How many other times had they been clients and not conquests? Her heart banged against her ribs with sudden hope.

'Look at me!' ordered Royce, a rough insistence in his husky voice. 'Do you believe me?'

She looked into his handsome face, caught by a strange gentle pleading she couldn't understand. It had been there so many times before, but she was sure she was misreading him. 'I want to,' she said warily.

'Then do. I admit there have been times when I deliberately wanted you to think these clients were—conquests, as you put it. But not any more. We've got to talk things out, clear up everything between us. Let's go now.'

She smiled tremulously, hope chasing dismay through her mind. 'I can't. Susan's taking Adam and Zack and Ryan to the baseball game tonight and I told her I'd be home early to watch Robbie.'

'What about Mrs MacPherson? She could watch him just this once.'

She shook her head, remembering how grateful the housekeeper had been when she had told her to take the evening off. 'No one was staying home tonight except me, so I told her she didn't have to stay either.'

'Kathleen?' He looked at her hopefully.

'She's gone sailing with Charles Hyland. I don't expect her back much before midnight.'

Royce dragged his hands through his hair in distraction, muttering angrily before letting out a ragged oath. 'After dinner, then. I should be home by nine-thirty—ten at the latest.'

CHAPTER TEN

JENNA missed the bus she usually took home and the following one was more crowded and made twice as many stops as the earlier one. It was almost seven o'clock when she walked up the drive.

Susan was standing on the front steps waiting for her and quickly handed Robbie into her arms. 'I don't know why you insist on taking the bus,' she said on a wave of irritation. 'I could have picked you up and been home an hour ago.'

'I'm sorry, Susan. Call it my last stab at independence.' Jenna pushed away a fleeting memory of Royce's grim face when he had received that same answer to his same question right after they were married and he had offered to buy her her own car. 'I really didn't think I'd be this late. I got tied up at the office.'

'I told Royce we were going out tonight. Why couldn't he be more considerate and let you leave early? I don't understand him at all, any more. His mind is a million miles away.' Susan stamped her foot impatiently. 'We'll probably be late for the game and I wanted to tell you about Peter before he——'

'Come on, Susan! You can tell her Peter's good news later.' Ryan and Zachary ran down the steps and hustled her to the car. 'If we hurry, we just might get there before the third inning.'

'I'm really sorry, boys,' Jenna tried to apologise again as they sped past her.

'Don't worry about it, Jenna. It's no big deal.' Adam sauntered on to the porch and smiled at her before running his hand over Robbie's curly black hair. 'We won't miss any of the game. We'll be listening to it on the radio on our way——'

'Come on, Adam!' Ryan shouted. 'You can make eyes at Jenna some other time. We're going to be late!'

A red flush crept up his neck. 'I'm going,' he muttered angrily, turning away from her.

Jenna smiled sympathetically. They were always teasing him about her and she didn't know what to do about it. 'Have a good time,' she waved. 'I hope the Blue Jays win.'

With loud goodbyes and an ear-shattering blast of the horn, they disappeared down the drive.

'Well, Robbie, it's just you and me now. I wonder what your Uncle Peter's good news is?' She looked at her son and hugged him tightly. Peter had sent a letter from Mexico only last week, full of congratulations and best wishes for them and their newly adopted son. When Jenna had read it and looked at Royce with wary eyes, he explained coldly that he had written to him, telling him of their marriage and his adoption of her son. That way, he reasoned, he was warding off any unpleasant confrontations if and when Peter decided to come home again.

'No, I didn't tell him Robbie was his,' he said stiffly. 'I've adopted him. He'll stay mine.'

Jenna sighed and shifted Robbie in her arms. 'It's a good thing you've learned to walk. You're getting heavy!' She smiled at him and quickly went into the silent, empty house.

Only when Robbie had been settled for the night did she allow herself the luxury of going over every nuance of those last few minutes in the office with Royce. She had put it out of her mind all the way home, afraid to dwell too deeply on it. It had always been safer not to let herself feel anything where he was concerned. But now, everything returned sharp and clear and clamouring, and it only confused her more than ever.

If only she had more experience, more knowledge, maybe then she could understand this change in him. She could see it. She could feel it. But she didn't know what it meant. Royce looked like a man who had reached the end of his tether. For the first time in all these weeks of maintaining a polite, detached insouciance, she suddenly realised his face had become thinner, the slashing grooves more pronounced. His suits didn't fit him as well as they had before. Now they seemed to hang on his powerful frame. Only his eyes had retained their fire, and today she was sure they gleamed with desire for her.

But was that all it was? Was that all it could be? Her heart did a curious little somersault. Maybe . . . just maybe, he was falling in lover with her. So many times she had wished for it, achingly dreamed of it, only to waken and tell herself it was impossible.

She nervously twisted the wide gold ring on her finger and felt a shudder of apprehension slide down her spine. '*You're my wife,*' Royce had said with such passion. Even now, the memory of it swept through her and made her heart pound. Oh, please, let it be love!

And yet the more practical side of her mind cautioned her to be wary and not read something into it that wasn't there. Sometimes he looked as if he despised her. And yet at other times, she was sure she saw an odd glint in his eyes, almost a yearning, a shattering tenderness that left her weak and breathless and trembling.

She had misjudged him before, but it was a hard habit to break. Why would he suddenly fall in love with her now? What had happened to make him change?

With a wrenched sigh, Jenna pulled herself together and ran a hot bath, telling herself all this speculation was getting her nowhere. She'd just have to wait and see. When Royce came home tonight, they'd talk it out and then she would know where she stood.

The time dragged endlessly before she heard his car on the drive. She took one last look at herself in the mirror, breathing deeply, telling herself to calm down. She nervously smoothed her hands over her loose flowing hair and ran them down the sides of the simple gown she had chosen to wear. Long and white, it made her look virginal. If she was going to be totally honest, she might as well look as innocent as she was, she thought nervously.

A stereo unit was softly murmuring Brahms in the background when she slowly descended the stairs. The crystal chandelier in the foyer had been dimmed and Jenna thought she heard a low murmur of voices and the decided clink of glass coming from the softly lamplit drawing room.

For a moment, she hesitated. Then she went to the doorway and stood stock still, the smile of anticipation in her eyes dying as all the blood swiftly drained out of her face. She would have turned or backed away, but her legs refused to move. She could only stand there, stunned, trying to steady her breathing, trying to hang on to her self-control, clenching a tight fist against her mouth to keep herself from screaming.

Royce was sitting on the sofa with a gorgeous dark-haired woman, a fluted champagne glass in his hand. She watched him smile deeply into the woman's eyes and hold his glass to her lips. Image after agonising image flashed in slow motion before her stricken eyes. Soft red lips sipped the golden wine, then Royce turned the glass from her and put his own lips on the same spot and drank deeply, sensuously.

Jenna saw the manicured hand slide across his cheek, caress his ear, curl into the sensitive skin at the side of his neck, saw the provocative, inviting, voluptuous body in a startling black backless dress sway towards him.

A wrenching pain struck at Jenna's heart, slashing it to bruised and bleeding ribbons. Deep shudders racked her body as she stood there, unable to move. Her raw nerves twanged. Her body felt on fire and there were huge bright tears standing in her eyes. She couldn't breathe. The room seemed to rock and tilt and close in on her.

'. . . we shouldn't be doing this,' she heard the woman murmur huskily as Royce's hands ran compellingly over her back.

'I'm finally doing something I should have done long ago,' he answered, his voice thick and oddly ragged. 'Don't tell me it isn't right. I can't help myself where you're concerned. I want you all to myself, not just for tonight but for ever. I want to sleep with you and possess your body and your heart and your mind and your soul. You know you belong to me, Lydia. Say you'll stay. I'll get a divorce. That cold fish of a wife I've got will understand and let me go . . .'

An unbearable horror choked Jenna and the hand pressed against her mouth became as cold and stiff as ice. Her tears suddenly dried up and convulsive tremor ran through her, and then she was frighteningly still, pale, sweating, staring blindly, like a statue, at her husband's handsome profile in the dimness.

'. . . oh, yes, darling, yes!' The woman's beautiful face was flushed and radiant with sensuality. 'I love you! I love you!'

Everything ran together in a terrible blinding swirl before Jenna's stricken gaze. She felt herself swaying dizzily and all at once it became the most important thing in the world for her to keep her feet.

How many times had she longed to hear Royce say such things to her? And she wanted so much to tell him, *I love you too! So much so, I could die with the pain of not having you return it.* The words bubbled up harshly in her throat, but she swallowed them back with a wild thrill of panic. She'd never say it now. It wasn't her place to say such a thing. She had never been a real wife to him. She had treated him coldly. It might have been a protective reaction, but he'd never know that now.

He would divorce her and she would let him go

with dignity, without a word of complaint, without clinging or begging or crying. Cold wet fingers ran up and down her stiffened spine and a sickening nausea boiled in her stomach. She didn't belong here. She had always known it. Robbie did, but she didn't.

Deep blue lines appeared at the sides of her white lips. Her eyes became glazed and bottomless with the sure knowledge of the agony ahead. She would let Royce go to this beautiful woman. If that would make him happy, that was all that mattered. She would let him go. Somehow, she would find the strength to do it.

A slight movement out of the corner of her eye caught her attention and slowly, steadfastly, the harsh rigidity left her. She turned.

'Jenna!' Royce closed the front door behind him and saw at once that something was terribly wrong. 'What is it? What's happened?'

Her mouth fell open on a soundless sob. Her stricken eyes widened, then swivelled back to the drawing room. Royce was still there with that gorgeous woman, wrapped up in her, oblivious to everything, everyone else.

But Royce was standing here in front of her now, gripping her arms, staring into her ashen face.

She put a dazed hand to her eyes and blinked rapidly, swaying towards him, trembling all over like a thin reed in a high wind. 'Royce?' she croaked, feeling a sudden rush of salt water in her mouth. She swallowed convulsively and her icy fingers clutched at the front of his shirt. He was real, not some figment of her imagination. 'But— who——?' She turned back to the dim room and Royce followed her glazed look.

All at once his lips tightened and his face twisted. 'Peter,' he stated flatly.

Torment was stark in her eyes. 'I thought—Oh God, I thought—he was you——' All the icy barriers came crashing down. The high wall of stubborn pride and dignity crumbled to dust and she stood there in front of him, utterly defenceless and open and vulnerable.

'If it had been me sitting there instead of Peter, would you care?' he demanded with quiet incredulity. 'Would it make any difference to you?' His smouldering eyes examined every inch of her colourless face. *'Would it?'*

Her eyes clung to his and she knew if she answered him, her life would never be the same again. She thought of all the cold and indifferent pretence that lay between them and shuddered. It had been her protection and now it was gone. He had to know just by looking at her how much she cared.

But how would he use that knowledge? Would he take the only thing she had to offer him and throw it back in her face as an unworthy gift? He had so many other women, so many who were beautiful and accomplished and experienced, so many who knew how to please him, what to say, how to——

'Tell me,' he said in a tortured voice, 'do you care at all about me? Or is it Peter? Do you think of him every time you look at me? When you look at your son, do you remember how it was with him?'

She stared at him helplessly, trembling all over, her heart in her eyes. 'Oh, Royce, it was never Peter! Never—ever—Peter!'

Her voice must have risen on the choked sound of his name, for Peter looked up just then and slowly got to his feet, clearing his throat selfconsciously.

'Well, hello, Royce.' He came between them like a blast of icy wind. 'And you must be Jenna.'

For the life of her, Jenna couldn't utter a sound. A deep shudder ran through her as Royce's face changed and his arm came right round her, pulling her close against his side in a sudden protective gesture that made her weak.

As Peter came closer, she looked from him to Royce, back and forth, her head moving as if in denial. He only loosely resembled Royce. Tall and lean, Peter had the same thick black hair and straight nose, but under the light of the chandelier, she could see his skin was more swarthy and tanned and lined. He had the same grooves slashing the sides of his face, but they were not as pronounced as Royce's. He was much younger and not nearly as handsome. He wore a dark suit, much the same style that Royce favoured, but it didn't fit Peter half as well. His chest was not as broad, not as powerful, not as inviting.

Peter's face coloured at her unconsciously delving scrutiny. He ran his fingers through his hair and smiled faintly. 'You look surprised to see me. Didn't the kids tell you I was flying in this afternoon?'

She swallowed and somehow found her voice. 'There wasn't time. I was late getting home and they had to leave in a hurry.'

'They never change,' he said in mock exasperation. 'Always rushing off somewhere. They probably didn't tell you my good news, either. Our good news,' he corrected himself, motioning to the woman hesitating awkwardly in the doorway to come forward. 'Without you, my darling, I'd never have been made General Co-ordinator of Tenochtitlan's Great Temple dig. Lydia Melendez,' he proudly introduced her, 'this is my brother Royce and—and you *are* Jenna, aren't you?'

She nodded, breathing shallowly before glancing up at Royce.

Although he had greeted Peter and Lydia first, as politeness demanded, his eyes went straight to Jenna. Then, warily, he turned again to Peter, squaring his shoulders, unconsciously bracing himself, his eyes dark with suspicion. 'Has she changed so much? It almost sounds as though you've never met Jenna before tonight.'

'I never had the pleasure. She was always out when I visited Meg.'

'But you used to talk about her——' Royce bit off the rest of the sentence and looked at his brother with a silent question.

Peter was discomfited. Something was going on here, but he didn't have the faintest idea what it was. 'I'm sorry, Royce. Meg always told me Jenna was as pretty as a mud fence and I'm afraid, in those days, with my youthful arrogance, I merely repeated her descriptions. I was shocked when I heard you'd married her.' He smiled an apology at Jenna. 'I should have known you were beautiful too. Meg could never stand any competition!'

Something flared in Royce's eyes. 'Excuse us, Peter, Lydia.' He urged Jenna towards the stairway. 'I haven't checked on my son yet tonight . . .' His voice trailed away as he took the stairs two at a time, pulling a breathless Jenna after him.

He didn't stop until he reached her bedroom, practically dragging her inside. He firmly closed the heavy door behind him and locked it before leaning back against it, shaking, his arms folded across his broad chest, his eyes darkly grey and burning. 'Now, Jenna, start talking.'

Her lips trembled as she nervously twisted her hands together in front of her. She had to have time—time to gather her scattered wits, to regain her composure, to figure out how best to even begin to explain. Breathing deeply, she tried to drag her eyes away from his, but he moved suddenly and grasped her shoulders, stiffly holding her at arm's length with hands that became tight iron talons.

'Oh no, you don't! Not this time. You're not retreating behind that damned great wall of ice now. I've got to know. Tonight you saw Peter with his girl-friend and you thought it was me. Your face was as white as death. Does that mean you care?'

'You were very rude just now——' she began, trying to twist out of his grasp, but his crushing grip tightened.

'Rudeness be damned! I want you to tell me. Do you care at all about me?' He began to shake her unmercifully.

'Yes!' she choked, goaded into the admission. 'Yes, I care. I have feelings too. But you never knew that, did you?' Her bitterness reached out to him and he jerked his hands away from her as if she burned him.

Her words went on striking him like lifeless stones. 'Have you any idea how demoralising it is to sit here each evening, listening to your family sing your praises, while all the time I'm picturing you in the arms of some beautiful woman? I make their dinner reservations, send them roses, choose their jewellery——' Her voice sobbed. 'I'm your wife, yet I have no place in your affections. You're merely paying me to do a job. I knew the terms before you married me, and I've tried to accept them. I've tried to be your paragon.' Her voice was bitter but she lifted her head, unable to abandon her pride completely. 'But tonight, seeing Peter, thinking he was you, I—I—Oh God . . .!'

Royce's hands fell to his sides defeatedly and a peculiar grey colour ran over his face. 'All this time I thought you were comparing me to Peter and finding me wanting!'

She jerked her eyes to his. 'I'd never even met him before tonight.'

He became very still, not moving, not even breathing, his relentless delving gaze suddenly making the blood pound deafeningly in her ears. 'But I thought you had, that you and he——' His mouth twisted and his chest rose and fell with ragged breaths. 'Then who the hell is Robbie?' he demanded so softly the hair on the back of her neck stood on end.

Her mouth was dry. 'He's Peter's son,' she said helplessly.

His head snapped back and a fine rage shuddered through him.

'But he's not mine,' Jenna gulped hurriedly.

His jaw clenched. 'Your name was on his birth certificate—I saw it!'

'Oh, Royce.' She pressed a shaking hand to her mouth. 'It was Meg—she put my name on it without my knowledge. It was her way of making me responsible because I'm the one who talked her out of an abortion. All the time she was pregnant, she kept saying she "had to get rid of it".' She shuddered. 'But I thought if she went ahead and had him, once she saw him, held him——' Tears began to sting her throat, choking her. 'But it didn't happen that way. She meant it when she said she wanted no part of him.' Jenna's eyes became huge and stricken, pleading with him to understand. 'And then you came home with her that night—and—and—looked at me as if I was dirt under your feet. I didn't want you to think—I was so plain—that no man had ever looked at me.' Her throat closed up so tightly that she could barely squeeze the words out. 'So I said he was mine.'

All the colour left his face. Instead of his usual cold hauteur, it was filled with anguish and his breathing became ragged and torn, strangling in his throat. 'If only you'd told me! God, Jenna, you don't know how many times I've wished we could start all over again. I never meant to hurt you, but from that very first night, everything I did or said only put you farther out of my reach. No matter what I tried, you wouldn't let me get near you.'

'I was afraid. I didn't want to get hurt.'

'When I found out about Robbie, I went crazy,' he grated. 'All this time—I thought you and Peter—I kept seeing you with him, kept imagining you and him——' He drew a shuddering breath. 'I never had to compete with him for anything before. I didn't know how to begin.'

Jenna backed away abruptly, staring at him, her eyes wide and incredulous in her startled face. 'You mean you were jealous? Of your own brother?'

'I thought you loved him. When I heard he was coming home today, I—— You're *my* wife. I couldn't let you go!'

She kept staring at him, unable to believe her ears. 'Are you saying you want me? *Me?*'

His face went stiff. 'I'm saying I love you, Jenna. I don't know how it happened or when. All I know is, there you were, in my office, and I kept saying the wrong things, doing the wrong things, and no matter what I tried, I couldn't reach you. All you did was give me those disdainful little smiles of yours.'

Icy shivers feathered down her spine. 'That was my only defence. Look at me, Royce. What right have I to expect a man like you to love me?' Her whisper was broken. 'The only women you ever look at are beautiful.'

'Oh, Jenna!' he muttered thickly, his arms helplessly held out to her. 'You've got a different kind of beauty I never knew existed—not until you got your hair cut and started wearing make-up. You looked like a lot of other women then, but I knew your beauty wasn't only on the surface like theirs. Yours goes all the way through. That's why I was so hateful to you and kept my distance. Every time I looked at you, I wanted to—— But I thought you loved my brother.'

She stood where she was, stunned, not daring

to move. 'But—all this time—all those other women—the dinner reservations you had me make—the *roses*!' She dragged her hands across her eyes and shivered.

'It was a ruse.' His mouth twisted. 'They were clients, that's all. I looked at them, but all I could see was my gorgeous wife. If I couldn't have you, I didn't want them.'

Jenna bit her lip, wanting to believe him—and yet . . . 'Meg?' she had to ask.

He sighed. 'I've been seeing Meg—with her husband—trying to smooth things out between them. From different comments she made, I found out about your promise to your mother. I only wanted to help you share that burden. I thought I had a right, as your husband.

'I only made it look like something else to try to get some kind of reaction out of you. My God, I thought you didn't care. You were always so cool, so efficient, so damned polite! How was I supposed to know you weren't saving it all for Peter?'

'There's never been anyone but you, Royce. Never anyone.' She was shaking all over and her shattered voice was barely audible as she took a tentative step toward him. 'That's why I was so upset the morning after we were married. I thought you knew—that you'd realised I never—— And you despised me for lying to you about Robbie.' Embarrassed, she started to turn away, but he caught her to him and pressed her head against his shoulder, holding her close for a long shuddering moment.

'There are so many misunderstandings,' he murmured into her hair. 'How can we even begin to correct them?' One hand came under her chin, tipping up her flaming face so he could read every inch of her enormous eyes, her full and tremulous lips, her skin flushed with fire. He started to tremble and a sound of urgency escaped him. She could feel him stirring against her. 'I love you, Jenna. I don't deserve a wife like you, but if you'll let me, I'll spend the rest of my life making it up to you.'

The floor rocked beneath her feet and a tiny gasp caught in her throat. She wasn't able to control the radiance welling up and through her. 'Oh, Royce, all I've ever wanted was to be yours.' But all at once her face changed as a horrifying thought struck her. 'What if—what if I can't—satisfy you?'

His arms came right around her, bringing her closer against his quivering body, holding her firmly yet gently as if she was made of some fragile substance before burying his face in her hair, murmuring incoherently.

When she looked up at him, his mouth burned over her face, drawing an instinctive response from her that left him dazed. 'Don't ever worry about satisfying me. You're more than I've ever hoped for.' He shuddered against her and she could feel the tremendous control he was exerting on himself to keep his desire in check.

'Royce?' she whispered softly, full of invitation, her heart thumping like a wild thing in her breast.

His breath stopped and he looked straight into her brilliantly flushed face. 'Now? What about Peter and Lydia downstairs?'

'Oh.' She was crestfallen. 'Do you think they're waiting for us?'

He grinned then and his whole face altered as he helplessly pressed passionate kisses on the warm length of her throat. 'Maybe not. They probably want to be alone as much as we do.' He glanced at his watch. 'And the others won't be home for an hour yet.' Love and desire leapt to his eyes and her face flamed when she realised he was only mirroring her own reaction.

'You look just like Adam and Zachary when they're up to something,' she chided, trying to hang on to her scattering dignity.

Royce threw his head back and laughed, his hands seeking the long zipper that ran down her back, causing all sorts of sensations screaming along her nerve ends. 'You can't imagine all the things I've been up to—and now I find I needn't have bothered!'

She frowned, bringing her arms up to wedge a space between his body and hers. 'Like what?'

'You know that job Peter's so thrilled about?'

'You?'

He laughed and the sound was rueful. 'I had to do something to keep him in Mexico. I didn't want him back here, taking you away from me.'

'But he couldn't have,' she said softly, her face deepening with bewitching colour.

'I thought he'd try. I pulled a lot of strings to keep him out of the way. So what does he do the minute he's promoted? He comes high-tailing it back here to tell us all about it.' His shoulders shook with a wry laugh.

'He doesn't know you arranged it?'

'He thinks Lydia's at the bottom of it, and from the looks of them tonight, it suits her fine.'

'He's in love with her, you know. I heard

him say he was going to ask his wife for a divorce.'

He sighed and just for a moment a resigned frown crossed his face. 'Maybe Melanie will be better off without him. She wanted children and a husband with a nine-to-five job. But Peter never wanted to be tied down that way. They've argued about it ever since I can remember.'

'Then you're not going to tell him about Robbie?'

'He's our son, my love. He belongs here with us. We love him and want him in a way Peter and Melanie never could. No one but my mother and your sister will ever know differently.'

'Our eldest son,' Jenna smiled rosily, the blood singing in her veins. Her fingers tugged at his tie and her smile widened when the silky knot came undone. It went sailing on to a chair along with his jacket. Her heart banged uncomfortably against her ribs when she daringly undid the buttons on his shirt, tossing it lightly to join the rest of the small pile.

Her hands ran in a feather-soft caress over the clenching muscles of his chest toward his stomach. When they touched the buckle of his belt, she lost her nerve and simply stood there, shaking, wild heat running over her body, her breathing shallow and jerky, her eyes unable to lift to his.

'Don't stop now,' Royce murmured, his voice oddly thick. 'This is just getting interesting.'

'But I—I——' She tried to gather her composure but failed miserably. What if she failed him now? When it came right down to it, she didn't know what to do.

'Jenna?' he said softly, unsteadily, pulling her shaking hands up against his chest where his heart thundered. 'I love you.'

Then his mouth twisted sensually as he slowly lowered it to hers and she forgot all her fears and let her instinct guide her along the path of love.

She needn't have worried. She was, after all, a paragon.

Harlequin Plus

A WORD ABOUT THE AUTHOR

Maura McGiveny describes herself as a "plain, ordinary, extremely shy housewife living in a suburb of Detroit, Michigan, with my dear husband and two young sons." Two things about her are extraordinary, though: her imagination and her stubborn streak. The first enables her to create the characters, settings and plots of her novels. The other made her stick to her guns when success as a writer seemed an impossible, fading goal.

She was first bitten by the romance bug when she was ten and read *Jane Eyre*. Years later, her mother introduced her to Harlequin. She was already a mother herself by then, but not too old to enter the magic world she found in her first Harlequin book.

There followed years in which Maura was unsure whether she should even try to write, let alone hope to someday be successful at it. But the urge was there, and she followed it. One day, the "impossible" happened: her first acceptance.

At the moment, she still considers her writing a hobby, but she has hopes—perhaps when her children are older—to make it a full-time career. She believes that as a romance writer she may now and then be able to "restore a reader's faith in the rightness of love."